stories of

passion and

dark fantasy

MENagerie

KYLE STONE

THE BACK ROOM

TORONTO, CANADA

The Back Room
is an imprint of Baskerville Books.

MENagerie
© 2000 Kyle Stone

"Aquamarine" appeared in the anthology *Happily Ever After*, 1996
"Chops and the Stiff" appeared in the anthology *Noirotica*, 1996
"Hot Stuff" appeared in the anthology *Hot Bauds 2*, 1996
"Master Class" appeared in *In Touch for Men*, September 1992, the anthology *Seduced,* 1993 and *Fantasy Board* 1994
"MENagerie" appeared under the title "Caged" in *Honcho*, August 1997
"The Pick-Up" first appeared in *Brief Tales*, reprinted in *Canadian Male*, May 1997
"Sexual Warrior" appeared in a slightly different form in *The Citadel* 1994
"Something About the Light" appeared in the anthology *Seductive Spectres,* 1996
"Touch Me" appeared in *Hot Bauds 2*, 1997
"Watching" first appeared in the anthology *Bizarre Dreams,* 1994

Canadian Cataloguing in Publication Data
Stone, Kyle
    Menagerie: stories of passion and dark fantasy
ISBN 0 – 9686776–1–4

1.   Homosexuality, Male - 1 Title

PS8587.T6628M462000   C813'.6   C00-930794-X
PR9199.3.S8216M462000

Cover photograph by Jayce Mirada
Cover and interior design by Kevin Davies

Published by:
Baskerville Books
Box 19, 3561 Sheppard Avenue East
Toronto, Ontario, Canada M1T 3K8

www.baskervillebooks.com
Kyle Stone can be reached at Kyle-Stone@baskervillebooks.com

MENagerie

Rows of giant cages lined the winding red brick path. Sunlight glanced off the bars and glistened on the skin of the naked men who paced about inside or lay listlessly on the straw pallets under the dappled foliage. Of course I'd heard about this place, but I'd thought it was only idle gossip, wishful fantasies spun by lonely men around the electronic camp fire.

"It is pleasant, yes?" My host gestured to the long row of cages with both arms, his smile splitting his dark face, his gold eyes blank and unreadable.

"It's... beyond words," I said carefully. Surely he knew it was repugnant to me to see my own kind caged like this, enslaved like dangerous wild animals. But I was a guest here. This was a diplomatic mission and my own opinions were not important.

In the cage to our right, under a tree that had been stripped of its branches, two muscular hairy men wrestled on the smooth grass. They were well matched in size, their broad backs both covered in black hair, their great arms straining as they rolled about, grunting like animals in heat. Even their asses were hairy, though less so then the rest of them. I watched in fascination as a third man walked over to them, tugged at his cock and started pissing on the wrestlers. The stream of urine steamed in the heat, matting the hair to their backs and shoulders.

"This one has given us much trouble," my host said, stopping outside one of the cages to our left. "A pity. He is a beautiful specimen."

"Indeed." My voice almost gave out as I looked at the 'specimen'.

The caged man lay on his back, his long tawny mane of hair half covering his face. His chest was well developed, his stomach hard and muscled. Apparently everything but his head was kept shaved, since his crotch was as smooth as his hard ass, showing off his cock and balls clearly. As we looked at him, he stretched, the muscles on his shoulders rolling. He got to his feet and paced over to us, his eyes fixed on me. Involuntarily I backed up.

"He has fire in his eyes," laughed my host. "We cannot douse that fire. And he has fire in his loins as well. A wonderful specimen. Such a pity he must be put down."

"What do you mean?" Startled, I pulled my eyes away from the naked man and looked at my host.

"He is not… fitting in." He sighed and turned away.

I glanced back at the man who was now stroking his cock as he watched me. Sudden heat flared in my loins and I felt the blush sweep up my neck and over my cheeks. A slow lascivious grin spread across his face. His dark eyes glowed, hard and knowing. His cock began to stiffen. As I watched, fascinated and appalled, he walked up to the bars and pushed his cock between them, right at my crotch. Without my volition, my hand moved to touch him. At once, he seized my wrist and held it in a human vice. Anger flared like wildfire in his eyes, searing my soul. I opened my mouth to protest, to defend myself. He spat in my face.

My host turned back to speak to me at that moment and cried out in alarm. He pushed a button at the side of the cage and a high pitched clangour filled the air. A moment later, two figures covered in shiny red protec-suits crashed through the door at the back of the cage, holding what looked like a great water hose between them. They aimed it at the man. He flinched as a single hard stream of pale liquid hit him in the back. His hand began to tremble, but he held me fast. Gradually he slid to his knees, his cock still stiff, the veins swollen. His eyes glazed over and at last his fingers slipped from my wrist.

I stepped back, stunned. "That wasn't water, was it?"

"Water? Against a wild animal? Certainly not." He smiled and took my arm and began to describe the banquet we would have tonight, before I would leave for my home base. My stomach churned at his loving description of the alien food. For a people who could no longer perform the sex act, these men had certainly not lost the ability to orgasm over other sensual delights.

That evening, I dressed carefully for my final official event. I was already longing to get back home to the base where I could speak my mind again with freedom and touch a man with desire, without the fear of being thrown into a cage and used as entertainment.

"What do you know about the menagerie?" I asked Ghalin, the young man who had been appointed to help me prepare for the banquet. My hosts had seen to it that I was never alone, another nerve-racking custom of theirs.

"Not much." He shrugged his elegant narrow shoulders. "We do not have menageries in the provinces," he said. "It is a great lack."

"So you enjoy the caged men?"

"Of course. They are beautiful, and so full of the drive to have sex." He shook his head in wonder.

"What do you do—have parties that go to the zoo and watch the animals mate?"

He smiled tentatively, sensing my anger, but not understanding it. "But they enjoy it too. Where is the harm?"

"The harm?" I clenched my fists at my sides and willed myself to calm down. "Where do the men come from? The ones in the cages?"

"They are sent here. It is all legal." He tilted his head to one side, his golden eyes warm. "Are you ready to go to the Hall, now?"

All through the long intricate dinner ritual I kept thinking about the men in the cages. Ghalin was a naif from the provinces. He wouldn't have any real information. But something he had said stuck in my mind. *They are sent here.* Information they were fed to explain the horror? Or was there some truth in it?

When the meal was finally over, my host escorted me through a long hallway to a pleasant enclosed garden. A water fall tumbled down rocks into a basin at one end. One section of the water flowed over part of a glass-like cube about eight feet high and ten feet square. Some of the guests were already wandering over to look into the cube. They laughed and gestured. One of them touched his loins and smiled at me over the heads of his companions.

"What is it?" I asked, turning to my host.

"Our after dinner entertainment," he said. "I saw how interested you were in the menagerie, and especially in the one we call Dharl. Come. Let me show you."

As I followed him, I wondered if Ghalin had told him what I had said.

When I got closer, I saw the cube was made of some material that seemed to act like a two way mirror. Inside was the great tawny blond guy who had grabbed me back at the cages. He seemed totally recuperated. He was pacing about, his large shaved balls hanging low. Behind him, it looked as if part of the waterfall was sliding down the wall of his prison into a shallow bowl. The walls themselves appeared to be green opaque glass. He paused, sank to the ground and began to do a series of push-ups; both hands, right hand, left hand. He was indeed in remarkable shape. Every muscle was highly defined. His ass rippled. Sweat glistened on every bronzed curve of him. It was clear he had no idea he was being watched.

Abruptly, in the middle of a squat, he leapt to his feet and stared at the waterfall. The wall parted and another naked man was pushed inside the glass cage. The wall slid shut behind him. This man was young, dark, lithe. He seemed a mere youth beside the gloriously muscled tawny god. He looked confused, then relieved. He said something. The other answered. He looked angry. The youth backed up.

"Why can't we hear what they say?" I asked.

"Why would we want to?" he said. "It would only be distracting." His eyes were rivetted on the dark youth's cock.

I pushed down my growl of frustration and turned back to the two men. The younger one held something in his hand. He was smiling, a sly smile, I thought. He opened his palm and the tawny god stared at the green jelly-like cube. He shook his head in anger, but apparently he couldn't resist the lure of what was offered. He reached out and grabbed the cube. His hand was shaking.

"What is it?" I whispered.

"They love it," he said. "We call it *yayne*. They do anything for it. And after they eat it, it makes them... aroused." He laughed, a high titter that betrayed his own excitement. "See? The dark one is already becoming tumescent. He was fed before being brought here."

A drug. I should have guessed. In spite of my disgust, I couldn't take my eyes off the pair. I was dimly aware of the others pressing close but all my attention was focussed on Dharl. He began to circle the younger man, his eyes glazed with lust. One hand touched his swelling cock. His lips were parted and he was obviously panting. They turned and lunged, wheeled and grabbed for each other. They were both slippery with sweat, but the big man had the advantage and soon he had the other man down, pressed to his knees. In one smooth movement, Dharl flipped him so he was on all fours, facing towards us. As if recognizing his defeat, the young man hung his head and offered his ass to the victor. With a snarl, Dharl grasped the suppliant's hips and thrust his swollen penis between the younger man's buttocks. The dark head snapped up, the eyes large with pain, the mouth stretched in a rictus of anguish. Even through the thick glass walls, I thought I could hear his scream.

The men around me sighed and moaned, as if they could feel the man's ass under them. I was sweating, too, feeling my own cock throbbing between my legs. I shifted uncomfortably, aware that my hosts were taking covert looks at me, their sly glances sliding down to check my crotch. I wished I was allowed to wear their loose garb. My tight-fitting buttoned pants made my arousal all too obvious, and there was nothing I could do about it. I noticed more than one hand disappearing inside voluminous folds.

Dharl was riding his victim hard, his eyes glazed. The dark man had collapsed on the ground, his hair half covering his anguished face. As Dharl pounded into him, his prone body shuddered and slapped hard against the ground. And then Dharl came, his mouth stretched in a soundless shout that seemed to rattle the walls. Everyone around me exhaled, as if they had been holding their breath.

I felt weak and dizzy. I realized I was gripping the smooth cool wall with both hands to keep from falling. I straightened, trying to draw away, to salvage some vestige of my dignity, but the men crowded me on all sides, their eyes still fastened on the sweating sex-driven male animals in the glass cage. Drool dribbled from the young one's slack mouth. His body quivered, his haunches jerking spasmodically as he tried to rub his still swollen cock against the ground in an effort to find some relief. Come oozed from his ass.

The blond giant sat on one of the cubes, his legs spread, catching his breath. He leaned forward and with both hands, he scooped up water from the waterfall and flung it over his head and shoulders. His bronzed skin glowed. As we watched, his great cock began to swell once more, throbbing and jerking between his legs as if with a life of its own. The man on the ground saw it too and began to crawl, desperate to get away. But the giant merely laughed. Slowly he got to his feet and stretched. He reached out one powerful hand, grasped a handful of the dark man's hair. He lifted him half off the ground and dragged him to the cube he had been sitting on and flung him face down over it. Now the poor man's bruised buttocks were facing us and I could see some blood mingled with the come that dribbled out of his ass. The man beside me was breathing hard. I swallowed. Even though I knew what was coming, I flinched as the giant plowed into his helpless victim. The heat that swept over me was as intense as it was unexpected. I wanted to be in there! I wanted to be at the blond giant's mercy, to feel his great hands rough on my back, to be split my his monumental cock! A small cry escaped me as I pressed myself against the glass, feeling the hardness on my own swollen cock.

On the other side, Dharl's thigh muscles clenched as he banged the younger man. His shaved balls were tight, huge like a naked fist. When he came, his head snapped back and his whole body arched.

I was aware again of my surroundings. As I drew away from the glass wall, I saw Dharl kick his partner's ass several times, until the exhausted man fell off the square stool onto his face on the ground. The light slowly faded in the cube and I could see no more. Around me, my hosts applauded politely, as if at the theatre and began filing out of the Hall. Unsteadily, I followed.

It was a moment before I was aware of Ghalin at my side. "That was a most appropriate final performance," he said, rubbing his soft hands with pleasure.

"Final?" The word hit me, like a blow.

"It is unfortunate," Ghalin went on, "but as I told you before, he has become unmanageable. He has already killed one of his sex mates."

I thought of the crumpled body of the young man back in the glass cage, streaked with come and blood. And I remembered the green drug in the young man's palm, the way the blond's hand trembled as he reached to take it.

"We will be sorry to see you leave," Ghalin went on, as we walked together through the long curving hallways to my apartments. "I have been authorized to offer you your choice of parting Gift."

I knew of the custom. It was an honour to be

offered a parting Gift, but at the moment I was too unnerved by what I had just witnessed to give any thought to my choice.

As if reading my mind, Ghalin told me I could take the evening to think about it. Before leaving me at my door, he touched my hand. "Do you wish a companion for the night?"

I stared at him. His gold eyes stared back into mine, unblinking, unwavering. Was he offering himself? Or some other sexless creature like him? And how could I turn him down?

"You would enjoy the male Dharl, no?" he asked, his face suddenly sly.

I couldn't stop him from seeing the hunger in my face, even though I turned away quickly and pretended to pour some wine from the carafe on the table.

"I have guessed right, have I not?" he went on, his voice now merely a whisper.

"I don't deny I was attracted to him," I stammered, trying to find a way out of the predicament. "Too bad it wouldn't be safe."

"Oh I should think it would be safe by now," he breathed. "The males are sedated after a show. Otherwise they might injure themselves, or others, if they are not yet satisfied."

I didn't answer. I took a long time drinking the wine, pouring another glass, drinking that. A warm buzz rose unbidden from my groin. I ached for sex, hungered for the feel of hot flesh against mine. But there was no way I could allow myself to do this, to have intercourse with a man they had enslaved. That would be like agreeing with what they were doing. I was a representative of my people. I couldn't do that.

But it was almost as if he could read my every thought. He was beside me, now. Very close. I could smell the clove scent of his warm breath, the musk from his fine-boned body. The heavy sleeve of his garment touched my arm. For the first time I wondered what he looked like under all those robes and jewelled scarves.

"No one would ever know," he whispered.

I could feel the feverish intensity of his desire, forever unfulfilled with his own kind. Did he crave this as much as I? Did he, too, long to touch that sinewy golden flesh, to feel through me the pounding rush of hot sex?

I took a deep breath and tried to steady myself. His clothing stirred with a heat all their own, touching me on the arm, the thigh, the foot. He was too close.

"You'll be gone tomorrow," he whispered.

"I'd like to see the man. To talk to him. That's all."

"I will have to be there."

Of course. I nodded.

"Come with me."

I told myself I was only going to look, to talk, maybe find out some details about how this could have happened. I almost believed it, too, as I followed my slim companion down the hall to a door that seemed like part of the panelling. At his practiced touch it slid back and I went after him into the darkness on the other side. The panel slid shut behind me.

After a moment, I realized the place was lit by dim phosphorescent stripping that followed the line of the ceiling. The walls were so close together I could hear my guide's robes brush the sides as he hurried forward. We walked in silence for about five minutes. Then the floor sloped abruptly down and somewhere up ahead, I heard water.

"Where are we?" I whispered.

"Not much further," he answered softly.

He paused, touched another panel in the wall and led me out of the corridor into what seemed like a garden. A cool breeze swayed the tree tops and tinkled the silver prayer bells tied to the branches. I wondered how the men in the cages interpreted these prayers.

And still my guide moved forward, winding his way along a well trodden path through thick bushes. Judging by his silence and the stealthy way he moved, what we were doing was forbidden. I wondered how far my diplomatic immunity could be stretched.

Ghalin stopped at a heavy door in a stone wall. He opened it with a key he withdrew from some hidden pocket in his robes. How long had he been planning this? Inside, stone steps led down into a dim underground room. A blue/white disk in the middle of the low ceiling, cast its cold light on five small cages on wheels lined up on one side of the place. Naked men were curled inside, the bars pressing against their backs and buttocks, their shoulders rounded in the cramped space. In the cage at the end was our blond giant. He was squatting, his head hanging almost between his knees. He raised his eyes, trying to see me as I moved closer. Even in that abject position, he looked beautiful.

"Do you have the keys?" I asked Ghalin.

Without a word, he went to the wall and took

down a ring of keys and handed them to me.

I looked into the man's eyes. They were clear of the glaze of drugs, now, but they still glowed with a subdued fire. The man knew no fear. I unlocked the door of his prison and stood back.

Ghalin gave a little gasp and stepped quickly behind the heavy grill that fit across the opening to the stairs as the man crawled into the open. Slowly he stood to his feet, rolling his shoulders. I felt his power in the air between us, his sexual energy reaching out to me across the small room.

"It took you long enough," he said. His eyes flicked to Ghalin, who stood with his face pressed against the grill. "Get rid of that."

I gestured to Ghalin to move back. The robed figure glided into the shadows.

"I know why they brought me here," the man said. "I am going to die, and I'm glad. But I want to be with a free man just once before I go, someone who wants me, who is not strung out on that green shit they call *yayne*."

"You can escape," I said, the words sounding childish even to my own ears. "Maybe I can—"

He shook his head. His full mouth curved into a wry smile as he stood there, regal in his nakedness. I felt my heart knock in my chest. "Come here." His big hand pulled me to him. I smelled the tangy musk of his body and felt my bones melt. His muscled arms held me against his gleaming chest and I reached for his head, holding his face between my two hands as I kissed him with sudden fire.

After a moment he pulled away. "We don't kiss

here," he said.

"Why?"

He shrugged, his big hands reaching up under my shirt, finding my nipples.

I caught my breath and leaned into him, my own hands running down his knotted thighs, spreading against his muscled ass cheeks. My desire for him mingled with a sense of anguished loss, even as I knew my body would possess him. But under his hands, my power seemed to drain away and in the end, it was I who willingly lay back against the cage and spread my legs for him, my trousers flung forgotten on the floor.

In the cold clinical light, his swollen cock looked enormous, like veined marble, and for a moment, I was afraid. By now I knew the taste of his flesh, the pulse and feel of every vein of the man's sex, as he pulled it dripping from my eager mouth. The big man clamped his hands on my ass and dragged me closer, until my ankles rested on his broad shoulders. I felt the tip of his penis nudging against my asshole. He paused. Neither one of us moved. I felt the bars of the cage rigid against my back. I looked up into his face and felt a sudden chill.

And then I screamed. I was split in two, impaled on that great cock, as helpless as a pig on a spit; just like the dark youth who had been part of our after dinner entertainment.

The man's face was suddenly one inch from mine. "The grand finale, asshole," he hissed. "And I'm gonna enjoy it!"

He pulled out and I thought my insides would spill on the ground, but at once he lunged into me again. My screams bounced around the low ceilinged room, mingled with his panting grunts and snarling imprecations. My guts were on fire, my back bruised as he banged into me again and again, my face wet with tears. Blood smeared his cock when he finally withdrew.

He stood looking down at me for a full moment, while I tried to steady my breathing. His great chest heaved. Sweat gleamed on his face and shoulders.

"Freedom," he said at last. "What a laugh." He reached down and scooped me up in his powerful arms. I thought he would dash me against the rocky walls of the cave, but stunned with pain, I was powerless to defend myself. Instead, he laid me down on the ground by the grill.

"You got a nice tight ass," he said. "Tell them the condemned man had a hearty final fuck." He laughed and walked away into the shadows.

I reached for the bars and pulled myself upright. I could see my guide rearranging his robes on the other side. Without a word, he took off his cloak and put it over my shoulders.

"In a few hours, he will be dead," Ghalin said.

I knew he would never understand why I did not return his wide smile.

working

late

I stand at the door, transfixed by the sight of Phil Galeano squatting precariously on the copy machine with his pants around his ankles. He sways as the white light beneath him slowly flashes over his pale ass and another copy of his spread cheeks spits out into the tray.

"Kiss my ass," he mutters. "Just kiss my sweet ass, you whore. You tramp."

"Phil, are you okay?"

"Oh yeah, sure, right," he shouts, and topples off the machine into my arms. The water bottle he was holding falls to the floor. I suspect it has more vodka in it than Evian.

Although Phil wandered into my fantasies from the

first day he arrived in this office, this is not part of the scenario. For one thing, I prefer my boyfriends more or less aware of me when we have sex. For another, I'm pretty sure Phil is straight. Still, as I hold him briefly in my arms, I savour the feel of his solid body against mine. My hand accidently strays to his warm hairy ass. I snatch it away.

I prop him upright and try not to stare at his surprisingly long cock. His legs are hairy and I can smell the sweat from his groin as I back away.

"Chris walked out on me last night," he says, making a pass at the ersatz Evian and nearly losing his balance again.

"Ah," I say, handing him the bottle. That explains his abstracted air all day, the refilling of the Evian, the many phone messages that were never returned. My desk is across from his and I notice these things.

"I'm sorry." I'm feeling inadequate. I glance at the open door of the copy room. It's late, but the cleaning staff might be around. I squat down and try to pull up his underwear. He's wearing purple Calvin Klein briefs, which is a surprise. As I work them up his muscular legs, the heat leaps from his body to mine, rushing through me like a grass fire, staining my chest, my neck, my face. So much for being cool. I must be beet red by the time he takes over and pulls himself into his own clothes.

He has been talking but I haven't heard word one. His black hair curls over his ears, falls untidily over his forehead. His hands are large but oddly delicate. "Shit," I say and turn away, walking to the plate glass window that overlooks the street twenty-two stories below. I freeze. Across the narrow canyon of night, the office opposite is lit up and a man leans against the glass, his fly undone, beating his meat as he watches Phil struggle to get decent.

"You perv," I mutter, though he is only doing exactly what I want to do myself—watch Phil while I close my hand over my own swelling cock.

"I don't know why I care so goddamned much anyways," Phil is saying as he struggles with his silver belt buckle.

"I better get you a cab." I look at his rumpled jeans, his t- shirt wet with spilled vodka. Our office of twenty somethings—graphic artists, programmers and animators—is pretty laid back but this is ridiculous. I steer him away from the window and whip out my cell phone. As I give our address, I watch Phil try to tuck in his shirt and finally give up.

"Dirty rotten walkaflex," he mutters and staggers to the elevators.

"It's a MidTown Cab," I call after him.

His answer is lost as the doors slide shut behind him. I turn around and look across the street. The window is dark. Disappointment washes over me. Down below, sirens wail into the distance.

Next morning Phil is subdued. He looks exhausted and I expect this time the water he drinks is real. He must be pretty dehydrated. He comes over, places both hands on my desk and leans in confidentially. I can smell the mints on his breath, the aftershave. His eyes are the colour of cream sherry.

"What?" I've missed whatever he was saying.

He clears his throat and leans closer. "Sorry about last night. I shouldn't drink."

"No problem." I lean back and smile up at him like an idiot. I need space. Breathing room.

"Did you.... I mean, did I leave anything...." He blushes and ducks his head. I feel something turn over in my stomach.

"I got rid of the evidence," I say.

"Thanks." He's blushing furiously and I swallow as he hurries back to his desk.

I waste the next hour not thinking about Phil, not visualizing my copy of his perfect ass at home in my bedside table.

Later on that morning we bump into each other in the copy room. That's where the supplies are and we both need diskettes. Before I can stop myself I tell him about our voyeur of the night before. He stares out the window.

"Bastard," he says. He's shaking with anger and humiliation. I see another side to him– that clenched jaw, the way the muscles stand out on his arm as he makes a fist and shakes it at the empty window. Carol, our head honcho, gives us a raised eyebrow as she picks up some blank CDs. I shrug and smile.

He turns to me suddenly and says, "Let's take early lunch."

"Sure." We've never had lunch together. The invitation flusters and intrigues. I grab my coat from the rack near the door and stumble after Phil. He walks with purpose, head down, hands stuffed in pockets. He doesn't wear a hat and I decide not to put on my toque, in spite of the cold. It's stopped snowing but our breath clouds in front of us as we cross the street.

"Where are we going?"

Phil ploughs straight ahead, leaping over the snow-bank and striding into the building opposite ours. Shit!

"Wait!" I skid after him, narrowly missing landing on my ass. He's already inside, looking through the building directory near the elevators. This lobby is bigger than ours, all marble and chrome. Two security guards lounge at a huge desk, surrounded by monitors. One wears a turban. He's watching us. Do we look suspicious? Out of place?

"What are you doing?" I hiss at Phil, tugging at his sleeve like a kid.

"Come on." Phil strides to the elevators, steps in and pulls me after him. The gilded cage purrs up. Phil punches the 22nd floor. All around us everyone is wearing suits and carrying briefcases. Some have laptops slung over their shoulders.

"I think we should talk about this," I whisper.

"This is it." Phil jumps out as the doors slide open at 22. I'm sweating in my parka.

Phil pauses a moment to get his bearings, then turns right and strides to the end of the hall. The black sign with gold letters proclaims Whiting Insurance Co. Phil bursts out laughing.

"Our perv sells insurance!"

"Maybe he wanted a piece of the rock last night," I suggest. We both burst into hysterics and stagger back to the elevators, holding on to each other.

On the way down, the cold stares of the other passengers sober us up. We grab a bite in my favourite pub a few doors down and I feel I have gotten to know Phil a lot better since the day before.

I have to work late. Again. I don't understand how the others get everything done so fast. I've only been on this job a few months, and I still have a lot to learn about some of the software.

Someone slips the Stones in the sound system. It's nearly 8:30 and I decide to pack it in. On my way past the copy room, I notice the door is closed, but light seeps out under the door. Curious, I stick my head inside and there's Phil, standing in the window, slowly gyrating to the old Stones hit: "Can't Get No Satisfaction". Mick growls and shouts. Phil struts and swivels. He's fully clothed, but I still want to come in my pants.

Phil starts taking off his shirt. He reaches back, grasps it between his shoulder blades, pulls it off, shakes out his hair. He twirls the shirt around a few times to the music, then tosses it over his head. It hits me in the face. I inhale his scent, a warm salty hint of sweat mixed with a faint whiff of cologne. I hold the shirt as I watch, mesmerized.

Phil is undoing his belt. Across the street I see our

voyeur, his hands flat against the plate glass window, his eyes wide, fastened on Phil, who now pulls off his belt and flings it in a corner. Phil's hips wiggle, gyrate. I watch his hand reflected in the glass as it slowly works down his zipper. He sways his hips side to side. With a final bump and snap the jeans hit the floor. He steps out, flicks them away with his bare toes and struts about. As he turns, he sees me. He falters, but only for a moment. He winks. He's wearing a silver thong. It's full to bursting and I feel weak behind the knees.

Phil backs up to the window and presses his ass against the glass. "Might as well give him a good show," he shouts above the music. He bends over, touches the floor, looks through the inverted V of his legs out the window at our voyeur, who is by now rubbing himself against the glass desperately.

Phil swings about and snaps his thong a few times. Then he glances at me over his shoulder and beckons.

For a moment I am paralysed. Then something gives inside and I leap forward, tearing clumsily at the buttons on my shirt.

"Take it off!" shouts Phil, strutting and posing, doing deep knee bends and high kicks that would make a Rockette proud. Where did he learn this stuff?

My hands are shaking as I pull off the shirt and fumble with my jeans. Phil bounces closer to help. He has worked up a sweat. His chest is damp, swirls of dark hair curling around his hard nipples. He touches my waist, his fingers firm and warm. He pulls. My 501s snap open in slow motion at his touch. They slide slowly to the floor. As I try to step out of them, I almost fall, but Phil catches me. Holds me. Puts his lips over mine. I don't hear the music any more. I don't see our spectator across the way. I am aware of nothing but Phil. His smell. His touch. His heat pulsing now through me.

Together we sink to the floor. My feet are still tangled in my clothes but it doesn't matter. I kiss Phil deeply, losing myself in his taste. His five o'clock shadow rubs my cheek and I moan.

"But... Chris?" I stammer.

Phil looks at me, perplexed. "What about him? He's out of my life. And I'm glad."

I kiss him again, so he can't say anyone else's name. Especially not that whore. That tramp, Christopher.

Phil rolls me over and pulls me up so I am on all fours. I am panting, starved for air, for Phil. I look over and watch him take a condom from his jean pocket, unwrap it, roll it on. He is hard, his cock long and glistening in its sheath. I shiver with anticipation.

He sucks the back of my neck, nibbles on my flesh, a spot no one has touched for a long while. I feel his cock nudging my ass, pushing between my cheeks. Finding my eager hole. I whimper with pleasure and push back against him, forcing him in. He thrusts once. Twice. I cry out and pant, trembling as he fills me. He pauses, lying against my back. We are joined.

I have lost track of time. Phil is now pumping steadily, faster, faster. When he comes he shouts and laughs. I shudder. I come all over Phil's t-shirt and one of my shoes. We slide into an exhausted tangle on the rug. I lie with my head on his chest, panting.

The music has stopped.

"Look," Phil says, pointing to the window.

I raise my head and look and see our insurance salesman collapsed on the floor with his pants down. He is pressing a paper against the glass with a phone number on it in magic marker.

"Bet this will keep him working late for weeks," I say.

Phil laughs,. "Me too," he says. "What about you?"

I turn away from the window and look into his eyes. "Maybe next time we could work late at my place," I suggest, watching him closely.

For a moment there is stillness in the room. Only the faint hum of the copy machine, looming large against one wall.

"Sounds good to me," Phil says.

I glance once more at the window. Our forlorn friend has gone. He has brought us together. I'm glad we gave him a good show!

something about the light

Living with Alisdair this past six weeks has changed me. Sometimes I feel as if I'm merging into him, becoming a part of him. I'm so attuned to his every move. I can feel his touch before his hand reaches me. It's like living in a sense of heightened awareness. Even the colours around me vibrate more strongly when he is near. Perhaps he is bringing out things in me I never knew were there. He's older. Wiser. And he looks like he models for *GQ* or something, the way his hair, touched with silver, falls in perfect wings over his ears. Broad shoulders. Trim hips.

I love the way his waist disappears into his jeans, leaving a tiny gap of air where I can slip my hand down into the warmth of his ass. I love the way his t-shirt reaches up as he throws the ball in the park, a pale alluring patch of skin winking at me. And his hands— I could croon on endlessly about the strength of them, the feel of them against my skin.

All the way to the cottage I watch those long fingers curling around the wheel, lightly stroking the ridges in the plastic, tapping out the rhythm of the music. I can almost feel the air stirred by his hands, pushing against me, caressing my hot skin.

Without warning, we burst through the blur of heat and trees and rock and below us lies the water, a tray of diamonds under the sun.

"And here we are," Alisdair says. "Almost."

He pulls the car to the right along a rutted roadway. Branches snap against the windshield and scrape against the sides of the car. Then the bushes open up and I see the place.

It's not a cottage as I am used to using the term. It's a house. An old rambling grey house with a wrap-around porch and many gables.

"Wow," I say.

"Welcome to Loon Lodge," Alisdair says, without a shade of irony.

"You didn't tell me it was... like this."

"I told you it was old. My great grandfather built it."

"Yeah, but you always talked about the family *cottage*. Like it was just a shack or something."

"Tim, it's falling down, for God's sake. It's nothing special, believe me. I'm going to sell it, remember? That's why we're here."

By this time we are out of the car and Alisdair is

trying to fit his key into the rusty lock on the back door. Vines almost cover the wall on one side and push up under the shingles of the roof. I wonder why Alisdair has waited so long to come here. Why he hasn't visited the place since his parents' death years ago.

The door finally relents and Alisdair pushes it open slowly, as if the air on the other side is heavy. He coughs.

"Bring in the stuff and I'll throw open some windows."

I trail after him, lugging the cooler. He moves through the house with a nervous energy that is new to him, banging open stuck windows, hammering back shutters, slamming open the doors upstairs. I trot back and forth bringing in the bags and boxes from the car, arranging them on the harvest table in the middle of the old kitchen. The linoleum on the floor is a pattern of yellow and brown squares, except for the part by the door, where it's blue. Willow ware plates gaze at me from the glass doored cupboards. Chipped mugs hang side by side with gilt edged cups. I notice a dish with Alisdair's name painted on it, a child's bowl. Somehow it all fits. I feel like an outsider.

Alisdair comes back, pulls up a trap door in the floor and disappears into the root cellar.

"Let's see if I can remember how to get all this started up," he muttered. I can see him studying an ancient-looking panel of levers and taps. It looks like something from a Frankenstein movie.

"Can I help?"

"Just put the food away. The fridge should be all

right. I called ahead to get the electricity turned on."

The pump kicks in. The water comes on with a strangled gurgle. I putter about the huge kitchen, stuffing things in cupboards. The fridge is prehistoric, but seems to be working. In a few minutes, Alisdair emerges triumphant from the cellar. I throw my arms around him from behind and squeeze, but he pulls away, still full of that nervous energy.

"I have to check the chimney," he says as he disappears out through the pantry.

When all the provisions are put away, I drift around the house, peering at the pictures and photographs that adorn every wall. There's a pile of old snapshots in an ornate box on a window sill. It's filled with sepia photos of several generations of Alisdair's family and friends. I recognize his younger self, hair streaked blond with the sun, laughing into the camera. I wander outside. Even with all the windows open, the air is close in the old place. Tall waving grasses slope down to the lake. I can see picnics spread out on checkered tablecloths, ladies in large straw hats and long dresses. The flower beds are a riot of colour, in spite of the weeds. I lie down on my back amid the blossoms and watch the clouds drift by.

Suddenly Alisdair bursts through the front door as if propelled by a great force. He stops abruptly, catching his breath. The sun lightens his hair. His face is streaked with dust, his eyes look deep and smudged. He seems older. I think; if I met him now, I would know he was fifty. His shirt hangs out and it's obvious he's used the shirt tails to wipe his hands. His feet are bare.

Suddenly he sees me, smiles. His whole face changes back to the one I know and love. He leaps on top of my sprawled body, knocking the wind out of me for a moment. My face goes hot and red.

"You're helpless, now! You're in my power," he growls.

I bat at him feebly, not meaning it.

He fastens his mouth against my neck, sucking like a vampire lover. I think of Tom Cruise and start to laugh. Cicadas sing loudly as he lies full length on top of me, pulling my hands above my head, pinning me to the earth. I smell his sweat and the dust in his hair and the hot heady perfume of the flowers. Laughter dies away into moans of desire as his body turns me on. He barely moves but I am aware of every inch of him, hot against me. His heart beats with mine, both speeding up slightly as our cocks swell, aching for release.

I wrap my legs around his waist and rock back and forth. The unrelenting earth grinds against me, tiny pebbles gouging into me. I don't care. I want Alisdair inside me, hurting and insistent, totally centred on the physical, the side of himself he had neglected for so long before I came along.

He rears back and fumbles at his waist, pulling a button off in his haste, unzipping his fly. I slide my nylon running shorts down over my ass. My cock springs to attention. I place my feet on his shoulders, my ass hole winking up at him, begging to be filled. Alisdair produces a condom from a back pocket, rolls it on with shaking hands. I'm amazed by how erotic this is, watching the thin membrane slicking his cock, the veins pulsing underneath. And then I close my eyes as he enters me, slow, sure, steady. He is panting now, gasping through his nose, expelling the air through his mouth. I buck upwards, my tears blurring his hot face, wanting to get past the pain. I know that at any second he will lose his concentration, will plow into me wildly, losing control in the only way he ever does.

He starts to keen, a rising wail of pure feeling. He is coming, his orgasm shaking us both. My own cock spurts, coating our chests, filling the air with the smell of sex and heat, mixing with our sweat. He lies on top of me for a few moments, catching his breath, pinning me once more to the ground.

I feel a shift in the air as he draws away; not so much physically—we still lie side by side—but as if his mind has moved away from me, back to the house, watching above us. I know I am no longer the focus of his thoughts, his being. I feel a shift inside, too—coolness seeping in where there was warmth, a kind a sadness in the midst of ecstasy. I have never felt this way before with Alisdair. I think about how to phrase this, to put it into words so he can explain it away, but he pulls himself to his feet and dusts off his jeans.

"Duty calls," he says. He looks down at me for a moment, an abstracted sweet smile on his face. The sun glints gold on the fine hairs on his arms. Then he is gone.

I gaze up at the grey house looming above me and wonder at the wistful sadness still lying inside like a spill of cool water. Clouds drift lazily past the many gables and peaks of the place. I see Alisdair at an upstairs window, fiddling with the green shutter, checking the hook, fastening it firmly in place top and bottom. He doesn't appear to see me. "It's nothing special," he said as we arrived. I don't believe that.

At last his industry makes me feel guilt. I get to my feet and start to collect wood for the fireplace from the woodpile at the side of the house. That much I can do without instruction. I can still smell Alisdair's cum on my skin. I can smell it on the logs I carry pushed against my chest. I imagine the smell rising though the chimney as we cuddle in front of the fire tonight, wrapped in each others' arms. I want him again. But he's busy with the house, cleaning the windows, replacing a pane of glass. I sigh and wander into the kitchen. I'll prepare a wonderful dinner for us both, use the candles in the brass candle stick holders I see in the cupboard in the dining room. It is usually Alisdair who does the cooking. This will be a change, a surprise for him on our first day in the ancestral halls.

After a late dinner, we listen to music and lie on our backs on the lawn and gaze at the brilliant stars. Alisdair tells me the stories about the constellations, and although I have read them before, it all sounds new and wonderful and special. We go swimming nude at midnight to Dolphin rock, halfway to Hog Island. Afterwards we make lazy love in front of the fire as the wind sighs through the pine trees. A single loon cries out across the water.

Although I assume that first night will to be different, I don't expect it to be the last one we spend really together. As the days pass, Alisdair has less and less time for me. When he isn't fixing the place up, he shuts himself away in the old music room with the pump organ, the scrolled upright piano and all the boxes of papers and books and family memorabilia he has collected there. In the evenings, he is too tired for much and our sex life dwindles till there is nothing much left but a quick morning fuck while I am still half asleep. I begin to resent this. I have the sense that I am fading—like the photographs on the walls, like memories of childhood.

One morning I shuffle down to the kitchen and look at the calendar. We have six more days left here. I am relieved. I want my lover back again. I look forward to getting home to the city. I'm even looking forward to my job interview. At least it involves me.

Alisdair is already hard at work in the boathouse, sawing and hammering, the air around him buzzing with dust. He doesn't need or want my help. I slip into my electric blue Speedo and wander down to the small beach. Off in the distance, Hog Island glows with a smudged green of lacy birch trees, the darker pines further back. To my right, a ridge of rocks beckons me. Alisdair mentioned something about caves before we arrived here. Since then, he hasn't said a thing about them. Today the memory of his words comes back:

"I used to go exploring around there when I was training for the swim team in senior high school," he said, a smile playing around the corners of his mouth. "It's... strange in there. Disorienting. Your eyes play tricks on you. Something about the light, I guess."

I strip off my t-shirt and measure the distance with

my eyes. I am a fair distance swimmer, but this will test my limits. The challenge makes up my mind for me. What Alisdair did at eighteen, I can do at twenty-five. I walk to the end of the dock, adjust my goggles and dive in, long and shallow. The sudden cold shocks my system. Exhilarated, I set out with strong strokes, churning through the green-blue water towards the rocks.

Almost there, I roll over on my back to rest. I look nearly naked. The wet Speedo barely covers anything. My sun tanned body is slick with water, my nipples hard. This close, the rocks loom high and craggy, sharp angles like giant blocks streaked with red granite, piled haphazardly along the shoreline. There don't seem to be any openings that could lead to a cave. Maybe things have shifted. Alisdair's senior year in high school was more than thirty years ago.

I have given up and am gathering my forces for the return trip, when I see the shadow of a gap between the rocks just under the water line. I take a big breath and plunge down deep, and slide my body through the opening. The surfaces of the rock are smooth and covered with lichen. The water is a darker green. I back up and come to the surface, realizing I will need more breath to get through the tunnel into the cave beyond. My finger tips are stained with green. I wipe one hand against my chest. Another breath and I am under water again, sliding through the narrow tunnel. It's like being born, I think. Or gliding into a Pharaoh's tomb, the walls on either side so smooth, as if sliced out of the rock. Ahead the channel narrows even more, then appears to open up. What if there's no air? Panic darkens my mind. My heart thumps, rising to my throat. I force myself on. I dive deeper. The light dims as I feel for the opening I sense is there. For an instant my ears are stretched with pain and I hear a man's voice. I can't make out the words. Just sound, deep, elongated, like a tape playing at low speed. My hands grasp the irregular ledge and I pull myself under the arch of rock, and up. Up. My lungs explode as my head bursts through the surface of the water. For a moment, all I'm aware of is the vault of a cave arching above my head and an eerie green light. I close my eyes and cling to a shelf of rock, as I gasp for breath. The air is different in here. Cool. Heavy.

A touch on my thigh startles me. Long fingers move against my skin. I gulp in air. Jerk away. The water splashes, the sound magnified and stretched out of shape. I pull myself further up on the ledge and my swimsuit slips. I stare at my leg. My skin looks dead white in the strange light. The water, disturbed by my struggles, laps noisily against the rocks, like laughter. Long strands of some plant, like thick green hair, undulate on the surface. The touch is insistent. As my breathing slows, I move closer, letting the green fingers caress me. By now my suit is low on my thighs. My cock floats free— languid in water, lengthening under the attentions of Aquarius. My pubic hair catches the light in some way that makes it almost glow. I pull off my suit with one hand and touch my cock, spread my legs, letting the cool, strangely heavy water touch me everywhere.

I have a sudden urge to open my ass to my watery lover, to suck the green tendrils inside me. I pull myself half out of the pool and turn on my stomach. The cold rock slides against me, then holds me in its harsh curve. Slowly I reach back and pull the globes of my ass apart. The water kisses my hole, pushes gently against the puckered brown eye. My cock touches the hard slime of the wall below me and my breath catches. Gradually the long tendrils touch the back of my thighs, trail higher, passing over my balls. I pull my ass wider, straining to make my secret places available to the chill probing of this alien hand. My hole reacts, opening and closing convulsively. I breathe in shallow pants, my whole focus on the sensation of touch, the slide of those long tentacles against my skin. My ears are filled with the gasping sound of my desire, magnified against the vaulted rock, twisted into an outlandish animal rutting noise that disorients me. I squirm against the hard embrace of the cave and cry out as a fat finger invades me.

"No!"

My scream reverberates around me. I slide off the ledge.

I come up sputtering and deathly afraid. The light seems to have dimmed. I realize I have lost my swim suit. Grabbing a gulp of air, I flip bare-assed into the frigid depths and swim desperately for the outside. When I surface again, I stop only long enough to fill my lungs and take off for home. My teeth are chattering. The light outside is dazzling. The sun hurts my eyes. I wonder if I'll get a sun burn on my ass.

Still far out from shore, I look at the beach and see Alisdair rising from the water, shaking his long hair, loping across to the log where he scoops up his towel and dries himself. From this distance, he looks young and vibrant. The nylon trunks cling to his thighs, leaving nothing to the imagination. I want him desperately. I need to feel his arms around me, his voice in my ear, his hands on my body. I call to him but he doesn't hear me. I throw all my energy into getting to shore. When I'm almost there, I look again. Alisdair has disappeared. Naked and exhausted, I crawl up on the beach. Now I'm glad I'm alone. I feel ashamed. Desolate. I towel myself off quickly, put on my t-shirt, wrap the towel around my waist. I make my way almost furtively through the long grass back to the cottage. I slink upstairs and get dressed.

This strange, disquieting mood throws a pall over dinner. I know I'm trying too hard, being too sensitive about Alisdair's preoccupation. Maybe that's why I feel a coolness between us that wasn't there before.

"I swam out to that cave you told me about," I say, desperate to get it out in the open.

"So that's where you were." He spoons warmed Cointreau over the sliced peaches.

"You're right. It *is* weird in there."

"It's dangerous."

"Aw, come on. I'm—"

"Jack Cunningham drowned in that cave." He lays down his spoon abruptly and looks at me, his hazel eyes glinting green in the candle light. "We used to meet there. It was the only safe place to be... alone. One afternoon we agreed to be there after lunch. My uncle arrived unexpectedly and insisted we all go to town with him. I had no valid excuse not to go. The next day I swam out to the cave to leave a note. I found Jack's body."

For a long moment he stares into my soul. I feel a chill slide down my back.

"Alisdair—"

"It was a long time ago." He picks up his spoon again and finishes off the sliced peaches too quickly. He pours the rest of the Cointreau into his glass and finishes that, too. "Do you mind doing the dishes? I have to get the wood under cover before it gets dark."

I jump to my feet, awkwardly scooping up plates and glasses. "About the cave—"

"Go there if you wish. You're an adult." He doesn't turn around, just goes through into the music room and closes the door.

I feel like a child, hot and frustrated, wanting to know the rules. This makes me angry. It makes the difference in our ages suddenly more apparent. In the beginning, it was just there. Now it means something. I see the ghosts crowding around Alisdair, blocking me out.

That night, I lie beside him in the old bed. It creaks as I move closer, trying to reach across the cool space between us. He turns away. I wait, watching the moonlight play across his shoulder, the skin silvered, otherworldly. Outside, a loon cries across the water. I shiver and move closer again, spooning my body close to his back. I know he isn't asleep. Somehow I can't bring myself to speak, to ask, to do more than let him feel my need as my cock probes against his ass. There is no response. Gradually I drift off to sleep and dream of cool caresses and a hot tongue on my throat.

"Alisdair, we have to talk."

We're sitting at breakfast, on the screened-in porch overlooking the lake. Alisdair looks tired. He's eating cereal out of the chipped ceramic bowl he ate from as a child, his name scrolling across one side in curling blue letters.

"I was thinking of staying up here a while longer," he says.

"But I have a job interview the day after we get back!"

"Do you really want that job?"

I am stunned. Getting that job has been the topic of many conversations between us. He's the one who has helped me hunt down just the right person to send the application to.

I feel that cool spill of melancholy spreading again inside me. I clench the spoon in one hand. I want to cry out: 'If you give up on me, I'm lost!' Instead I say, "Yes. I do want the job. It's right for me, Alisdair, you said so yourself."

"Did I?" He spreads honey on a piece of toast and looks out over the water before taking a bite, chewing thoughtfully.

"I want that job."

"I suppose I could give you a lift to town," he says.

"You could take a train up later and I could pick you up at the station...."

I don't say anything. It will take a while to assimilate all this. What does it mean? Finally I say, "So you're not going to sell the place?"

He shrugs and spreads his hands. "I don't know. Being here again.... I'm starting to wonder if it's the right thing."

So that's it. I get up and mutter something about walking to the village to pick up some lemons. I leave him sitting at the table, gazing out over the water as if I'm not there, as if seeing things I cannot see.

The long walk calms me and I return with the determination to stop worrying about a past I had no part in, a past so different from mine, that pulls at him because he is here, in this old house haunted by voices of his family and a long dead lover. I will pull, too. Away from this place and it's ghosts.

I'm hot and dusty from my walk. I'm feeling horny, too, but there's no sign of Alisdair. I change into my old bathing suit and wander down to the beach. The line of rocky cliffs beckons me across the water. What really happened there yesterday? *Something about the light....*

"Nonsense," I say out loud, sounding more like Alisdair than myself. I laugh and throw my towel on the sand and rush along the dock to throw myself headlong into the lake. This time, when I get there, I pull off my bathing suit and leave it on a shelf of rock, weighed down with a stone. I wonder if Alisdair and Jack used to do the same thing all those years ago. The

water caresses me as I slide down and through the hidden corridor to the secret chamber, bathed in its
strange aquamarine light. When my head breaks the
surface and I shake my hair back from my face, my
heart beats fast with excitement.

Gradually the pulse slows. It is dim today. I can
barely see anything. I wait. Nothing happens. No
water nymph-boy rises from the placid pool to warm
my goosebumped flesh. I pull myself onto the slippery
shelf of rock where I lay moaning with desire on my
last visit and look around the cave. Glistening rock
arches into blackness above me. A slick of green under
my left hand. I hear the drip, drip of water from somewhere out of sight. I am alone. I shiver in the clammy
air. My cock is flaccid, nestled on my lap.

Disappointed, I close my eyes and slide into the
water. The chill closes over my head. Just as I am about
to jackknife deeper, I feel it. A feather-soft caress on
my back. I freeze, drift back to the surface. When I
open my eyes, the light has shifted. Brighter. More
intense. The touch of the other has not left my back. I
dare not turn around or look back. I am afraid the
touch will withdraw and leave me desolate and alone.
I am breathing fast again, almost panting. My flesh tin-
gles with warmth. I reach out for the rock to keep from
slipping under and the surface feels warm to my touch.
I hear breathing by my ear. Something licks my neck. I
gasp, almost a sob, as arms embrace me, long fingers
flutter over my cock, touch my balls, lift them gently.
Another hand probes the crack of my ass. Blindly I
grope for something to grip, to pull myself half out of

the water. Everything slides away under my hands. Heavy breathing sighs through the cavern. Mine. Someone else's. A third hand pushes my legs apart, a fourth scrapes my left nipple, the one that is still tender from a recent piercing attempt gone wrong. My gasp echoes back to me, the magnified sound pushing against my ears. I struggle to pull myself up. The sound swells and I am suddenly face down on the shelf, my legs spread wide, my hole sucking at.... Something. Warm. Large. Like a penis. Like...Alisdair's cock.

I clutch the ledge above me and stifle sobs as I am invaded by this moist, muscular, penis-like thing. Beneath my prone body, the rock sways, holding me, rocking me. I feel as if the whole cave is making love to me. My ears are filled with sound. Murmurs and cries and the slap of water against rock. My own sobbing gasps. My cock is rigid against the shuddering stone. My cries become louder as I tremble and shake with orgasm. I call out into the roaring cavern.... A name.... A name....

I don't know how I managed to get back into the sunlight. I am exhausted. My cock is sore, stained with moss and lichen, my chest scratched as if by long nails. A drop of blood trickles down from my inflamed nipple. My mind is empty of thought.

After a while, I swim back home. Alisdair is waiting on the beach. His hair is damp, his swimming suit moulded to his trim body. Without speaking, he wraps me in a beach towel, kisses my lips. He whispers in my ear. He calls me Jack and squeezes water out of my hair.

I nod. I know I will stay here, now. I can't say it yet.

But I will. We walk back to the cottage, arms entwined. The porch door snaps closed after us.

touch me

I watch him every day. He's always there about this time in the afternoon, stretched out in a hammock slung between two maple trees. His skimpy faded red shorts ride low on his narrow hips; his darkly tanned body oozes sweat and lazy lustful sex.

I lie on my bed, looking at the mirror propped up on my window sill. I see him there, a cool reflection of the hot man in the next yard. I see my own naked leg, my arm moving as I grasp my quivering flesh in one hand.

"Touch me," I whisper.

I know he can't hear me, doesn't even know I'm here. I know that making the connection is all up to me. I watch him move his big hand over his chest, his fingers lingering on first one nipple, then the other. My own hand mirrors his actions. I imagine it is his sweat I feel, his skin slick under my touch. My ass wriggles against the knotted sheets. I hear my breath coming in short gasps.

"Touch me."

I flip over on my stomach, my chin just above the windowsill. He has bent one leg, his knee resting against the hammock. The wide leg of his running shorts falls back and I see the swollen stained cup of thin cotton that contains his cock. I swallow. My mouth is dry. I grind my own aching cock into the bed. The springs creak and strain. My heart pounds. My eyes are fastened on the man. I can almost smell him from here—precome oozing into the thin cotton, sweat gathered like honey in his arm pits.... I grunt and gasp. Come spurts into the dirty sheets.

"Touch me!"

My orgasm exhausts me.

When I raise my head and look again, he isn't there. My whole body shakes with sudden nervous spasms. I look from the open window to the mirror, seeking his reflection, at least. Nothing. I feel more alone than I have felt for some time, now. I look down at my naked flesh, smell my own come. I long for another's smells to mingle with my own. Now I have lost even the reflection of a desirable man.

A sound at the door startles me so much I can't open my mouth. Words are stuck in my throat. Clumsy, I try to wrap myself in the soiled sheets. I watch the door, mesmerized as it starts to open. I haven't had any visitors for some time. I thought everyone had forgotten me, moved on. I wonder what they will think when they see me, whether I will see the pity in their eyes.

I blink, clearing by vision. Sometimes the light plays tricks on me now. This time I seem to see the reflection of my man, but not in the mirror, not in the glass. He is standing in the doorway. I can smell the sun and the sweat and the sex. He is smiling, his eyes a hot summer blue. He comes in and closes the door behind him.

I relax my grip on the sheets gradually. They fall away. I feel his eyes on me, touching my dry skin, licking my parched lips. Now I'm afraid to speak, to break the spell.

He is standing beside me. He takes the mirror and adjusts the angle to reflect the bed. I see us both reflected there and what I see is his vibrant macho sexuality, my pale boyish aestheticism. I hadn't seen myself that way before. I know that he has no memories of my earlier, sturdier self, and I smile. He reaches down lifts the sheet away. My cock swells, looking bigger than ever between my slender thighs. Slowly, he pushes the waste band of his shorts down to his knees. His cock is short and fat, his balls heavy and covered with golden fuzz. I can smell the faint aroma of urine.

"Touch me," he says.

the

messenger

H e wasn't an old man, barely past his 40th year, but he walked slowly, as the old do. He looked ahead along the beach, his dark eyes almost drawing the details around him, the crag and rocks, the rhythmic roll of the waves falling over each other to break against the glistening pebbles far down the shore.

It was years since he had been back here, years since he had felt the tangy kiss of salt against his lips. Everything was the same, yet there were subtle differences he could just make out along the shore, details that didn't match the careful landscape of his memory. The old hotel had been pulled down, the post office moved. A row of cottages stood where he had played as a child in the long grass of the meadow below the lighthouse.

A year ago he had thought of himself as in the prime of life. Now, his world had slid sideways, and there was nothing to hold onto any more. After months of struggle and rage, followed by weeks of listless sorrow, he had arrived back here, almost shipwrecked by the uncontrollable swell of his emotions.

It was over. Here along the wild untamed coast of the Atlantic where he had come every summer with his parents, he had found peace. Or he thought he had, for a while. Now he felt restless, unsure, afraid. Perhaps he had given in, he thought, rather than accepted. His eyes followed the sweeping dip of a sea gull over the grey roll of the waves. He hoped the feeling of peace would return, leaving him free to finish his work.

The subject of his article was "The Messenger in Greek Drama". The one who brought the news, described the battles, all the stirring events too horrible to be shown on stage. All this the messenger recreated with his poetry, his memory so exact, whole speeches would be delivered verbatim.

The one who brought the news of his fate had used no poetry. Perhaps medical men should read the classics. Perhaps Greek literature should be a required subject before doctors could graduate. He smiled, imagining the reaction to this proposal.

He paused to rest and sat down, carefully adjusting his narrow buttocks onto an accommodating curve in the convenient rock, planting his feet against the smooth slide of the stones. The tide was turning. Far out across the expanse of pebbles on the beach, past the hulking mounds of rock, covered with their shifting coats of green-black seaweed, the mud flats stretched glistening in the cool sunshine waiting to be submerged again. Even as he watched, he could see the water creep closer, each wave eating more of the land between them.

His gaze moved out to the horizon, then back along the shore to the irregular granite cliffs that jutted far out into the water, cutting off his view. A bright shape flitted across his line of vision, seeming to be half in, half out of the deep pool of water at the mouth of the big cave. He blinked to make sure his eyes weren't playing tricks on him. Over the weeks, he had learned to distrust his senses, to test them again and again, afraid to slip into that shadowed land of unreality where every sound could suddenly take on a nightmare shape. He squinted into the distance. The figure was stepping carefully across the smooth rocks, head down, arms balanced out to the sides. A boy, it looked like, his long fair hair lifting around his head in the breeze. If this was unreality, it might not be too bad. The man laughed suddenly, the sound so unusual these days that it startled him, as well as a gull, perched on a piece of driftwood nearby. He turned as the bird rose shrieking into the clear sky. When he looked back, the boy, or whatever it was, melted into the shadows under the cliff. With a sigh, the man got to his feet and trudged up the beach, over the hills of pebbles flung up by centuries of tides, back to his small weathered cottage on the hill.

It was later that afternoon when he thought he saw the boy again, his fair hair on fire from the sun, the rest of him in the shadow of the wharf. The tide was in by now and the boy seemed to be standing in a boat. At least, that was all he could think of to account for the odd way that golden head appeared and disappeared in the deep cool shadows along the pier. On an impulse, the man stood up, pushing back the wooden chair that scraped along the floor with a shuddering noise. Absently, he swept his papers together, anchoring them under a smooth stone from the beach and started out the door. His sneakered feet slid in the long grass as he made his way down the hill and along the path to the pier. It was a hulking structure, left over from the days when scows pulled in to load the stacks of logs hauled in from the woods by the truckload. But that was years ago now, and the wharf was half in ruins. As his feet touched the wide boards, he was almost running, his heart beating a little too fast. But when he looked around, there was no sign of anyone. Disappointment washed over him and was smothered at once. He had come for a breath of air. He walked briskly to the end of the pier, where the boards became jagged, broken long ago by a hurricane that had tumbled and jammed the timbers sideways and upside down at odd angles. He watched a few old lobster boats, their wooden traps piled on the deck, bob quietly at rest in the harbor. Then he turned around and almost lost his footing. The boy stood right behind him.

"Hi. You want a ride?"

"A ride?" He felt stupid, staring at the young man

as if he had never seen a blond youth before. The eyes were startling, dark around the edges, dark in the middle, and in between flecked with green and blue, like the ocean. He looked away.

"I thought you came down looking for me."

"No. I just— Yes, I did."

"Good." The boy smiled.

The man felt a small explosion inside, as if his heart were suddenly on fire. He tried to steady his breathing.

"My boat's right here. I'll go first, if you like." He sped down the ladder, jumping to the deck of the old trawler with practiced ease.

The man came down much more slowly, taking his time. Now he could hear the engine throbbing softly.

"We'll go round the point," the boy said, casting off and revving up the motor. The deck shuddered under their feet.

"The currents are bad."

"I know the currents."

Odd, the man thought. He doesn't talk like a native. His voice was light, throaty, inviting. His gaze direct. Now that they were on the water, there was no question what he wanted. If there ever had been.

"Warm in the sun," the boy said, taking off his shirt. "We'll anchor around the point and go swimming. It's nicer there. More private."

"Are you in the habit of giving total strangers a ride in your boat?"

The boy shook his head, the shaggy golden hair flying about, electric with energy.

"So I'm your first?" the man went on.

"Hardly that." The boy glanced at him sideways under his long lashes, the look teasing, assessing, and something else beyond the man's experience. His bare arms were tanned, the muscles standing out hard as he spun the wheel, heading for the point.

After that, they said nothing, the boy intent on steering, the man content to watch the strong young back, the wide shoulders flowing down to slim hips, the stance casual, the weight on one leg.

"You're not from around here," the man said, finally, his curiosity getting the better of him.

"Neither are you."

Silenced, the man smiled and looked out at the horizon where the water met the sky in a grey-blue haze.

A few moments later, the boy cut the motor. In the sudden silence, the splash of the anchor was bright with new sound. The boy turned and grinned down at him. "The water's warm, here," he said. "It's like a small pocket of the Caribbean." He unzipped his jeans and slid them down over his hips, kicking out of them as he turned and climbed up on the narrow gunwale. His tanned feet looked long and delicate against the splintered wood. For a moment he hung there, naked and beautiful against the horizon. Then he dove into the gently heaving sea, leaving the man alone.

For awhile, the man watched the sun dance and beckon on the waves.

"No," he said at last, and turned his head away. "Not yet."

He waited for hours, until the boat was almost stranded by the tide. Then stiffly, he climbed out and waded to shore. He was smiling.

Adam

and Steve

It was meant as a joke gift, like the black rubber thong with the zippered pouch Chas had ordered from his sister's Fredericks of Hollywood catalogue for Jack's birthday. Jack had laughed and turned up the music and stripped right in the living room of his small crowded apartment, putting on a good show for Chas as he slowly eased down the worn jeans, then pulled off the socks, rolling the tight briefs over his hips and down his firm thighs.

"Don't move," Jack said, as Chas jumped to his feet and began to pull off his own t-shirt. "Not yet."

Chas sank back into the deep cushions of the old arm chair, his throat dry, his cock swelling to life as he watched his lover. Jack stepped away from the clothes pooled at his feet and pulled on the thong. His big cock was already hard to restrain behind the rubber pouch. Chas could almost taste the hot salty tang of the man as he watched the muscles flex on those powerful thighs, watched the dark hair on Jack's legs, the way the light from the one lamp cast delicious shadows where the zipper curved under to the tight hairy balls. He began to ease off his shoes, pushing the heels free with the toe of the other foot.

"Wanna try my zipper?" Jack said. He put his hands on his hips, his tits standing out from the encircling black hair like bullets.

Chas sank to his knees and crawled the few feet separating them. As he raised his head, he caught a whiff of rubber, mixed with sweat and the warm raunchy smell of unwashed underwear. Jack worked long hours as a carpenter. He had just arrived home when Chas surprised him. Chas drew in a lungfull of the man's scent. The odd blend of the real and the artificial, the sweat and the new rubber, was strangely intoxicating and Chas was driven to new heights of fantasy. He took the zipper in his teeth and gently pulled.

Jack's cock sprang out at him, hitting his forehead. Precome leaked down Chas's cheek and the younger man stretched back his head and opened his mouth wide, sucking in his lover's cock until he was full, his throat almost closed. He took a careful breath through his nose and sucked harder. Jack cried out. Chas could feel the veins pulsing against his tongue, the back of his throat. His own cock jerked and quivered as his nuts tightened. Jack pulled out and came on his upturned face.

"Happy birthday to me," he said and laughed and kissed Chas on his come-slick lips.

This time, the gift seemed to have misfired.

"Where'd you get this? The thrift shop?"

Chas bit back the irritation. "Remember that weird store I told you about in the lane running off Wellesley? I got it there. It's hand made."

"Yeah, sure. I hope you didn't pay too much for it." Jack tossed the large yellow gold candle onto the couch and went into the kitchen to get a drink.

Chas picked it up and held it a moment, running his thumb over the smooth naked figures of the entwined men. The longer he held it, the warmer the wax became, until the smooth surface felt almost like warm skin under his fingers. A strange tingle crept up his hand, running like fire through his veins into his heart. Startled, he almost dropped the candle.

"Another piece of tacky junk we don't need," Jack said from the kitchen.

"Fuck you." Chas moved into the hall and pulled on his old army coat. He dropped the candle into the large pocket and slammed out the door.

Outside the world was a Christmas postcard. The sun shone brightly, hurting his eyes. Clean white snow clung to the branches of the ornamental trees outside the apartment building and draped streetlights and fire hydrants. Great drifts of the stuff, freshly turned by the plow, was piled along the curb. Only underfoot did the picture perfect illusion disappear into the brown slush of a January afternoon.

Chas had no eye for the beauties of the day. He had left so quickly he wore only his sneakers and his feet were soon cold and wet. He lowered his head and crammed his hands into his pockets, plodding along the street without thought as to where he was going. His right hand settled around the waxed naked bodies in his pocket, warming his thoughts. Making him horny. In spite of the cold air, his skin throbbed with heat. He imagined Jack's thick muscular body, in nothing but his black nylon bikinis. He wanted to sink to his knees in front of him and let his tongue dampen the black material until Jack's cock swelled and thickened. Unconsciously, Chas rubbed the warm wax of the figures in his pocket faster. Faster. His thumb traced the small crack in the firm ass of one of the men. He heard himself whimper with desire and blushed, glancing quickly around to see if anyone else had noticed.

And looked right into the coal black eyes of a tall thin man, who stood watching him. Grinning. The man held his gaze and winked.

Chas couldn't look away. Nor could he stand there gawking. "Do I know you?" he said.

"Not yet." The man started walking beside Chas, leaning slightly towards him in an intimate way, shouldering into his space. "But that could be arranged," he said.

Chas walked faster. Something about the man frightened him, yet his closeness was almost electrifying. Chas could feel the air move against his cheeks, his neck. As they walked, the guy was so close now Chas was almost forced into the wall of the building they were passing.

To get away, Chas ducked into Starbuck's. The guy followed.

"Good choice," he said, with a wink. "What'll you have? A vanilla bomb?"

"Look, what do you want?"

"Shall we discuss it?"

"What's to discuss?" But Chas slipped off his coat and looked around for a place to sit.

"Grab a seat. We'll think of something." The guy ordered coffee, paid for it and followed Chas to the back. He sat down on the couch in the corner. Beside Chas. He was so close Chas could feel the heat from his body even through his coat, could sense the tension in the muscles of his thighs. He pulled the candle out of his pocket and threw it on the table.

"Nice," the guy said. "Adam and Steve. Where'd you get it?"

Chas shrugged.

"That one guy looks like you. Did you notice?"

"Yeah?" Chas leaned closer, looking at the waxen face of the candle man. It did look like him! "I never noticed!"

"Amazing what slips by." The guy dropped the candle into his lap, then picked it up and pressed it against Chas' growing erection. "Slippery little buggers."

"Look, I don't think this is a good idea." Chas squirmed. His face flushed and he glanced around feeling guilty, like he was a kid again, lusting after his unattainable swimming teacher.

"Stop thinking."

That was easy. Chas felt his body explode into sensation as the man leaned closer. His long black hair fell like a curtain between them and the other customers in the café. Chas gasped, and dropped one trembling hand to the candle. His fingers fell on the warm hand of the stranger, their skin melting together, like the wax that seemed to mould itself to the hungry shape of his body.

"Jack," Chas gasped, not knowing what he was trying to say exactly, only that at that moment, Jack was a part of his desire. "Ahhhh." His breath strangled in his throat. He was close to orgasm. Suddenly frantic, he pushed at the stranger's hands, shoving them away from the warm object between his legs that felt so much like Jack's insistent cock. His fingers closed over hard flesh. "Shit!" He scrambled back into the corner of the couch, like a child who had been badly frightened. The candle rolled onto the floor—nothing but wax. Reddish gold. Almost lurid in the bright breezy atmosphere of Starbucks.

The man leaned down and picked it up and tossed it idly from one hand to the other. His smile was slow and sexy, hinting at secrets.

Chas reached for his coffee and gulped the sweet creamy confection, almost burning his mouth. Around them the crowded café retreated into a blur of chatter and low music. All he saw was the dark man beside him, slowly, deliberately begin to lick the male figures fused together on the candle. All the time he watched

Chas, his eyes dark and hot. He knows I'm about to come in my pants, Chas thought.

The man shifted forward in his seat, blocking the view of the rest of the place. They were all alone, in their own secret corner. "You're going to come and my hands won't even touch you," the man whispered. Chas felt the will to move drain out of him. He wanted this man's touch. He craved it. He had to have it. His cock throbbed, straining painfully against his underwear. Chas pleaded with the man, using his eyes, his panting breath, his trembling hands.

The tip of the man's tongue touched the ass of the wax Adam, darting up and down the crack as his black eyes probed into Chas's very soul.

"Please..."

The man's dark laugh sent goosebumps up and down his arms. "Undo your zipper," he whispered.

"Here?"

"Right here. Right now."

Chas was trembling. He scrunched further onto his spine and worked down his zipper, his hand shaking. The man was sitting with his back to the coffee shop, shielding him from the curious, but at any moment someone could walk up to them, want the table opposite them, see his shame. Nevertheless, Chas did as he was told. All he could see was the great dark stranger, whose voice and eyes so hypnotized him.

"Pull down your jockies."

"But—"

"Do it." He hadn't raised his voice. He didn't have to.

Chas caught his breath and raised his ass from the seat, working down his underwear as unobtrusively as he could. He felt his face hot with shame as his swollen cock sprung free.

The man smiled, watching. "Sit on your hands," he whispered.

Chas did. He was sweating now, his whole body thrumming with sexual energy, begging for release, totally vulnerable to this stranger whose name he didn't even know.

The man gave one final lick to the wax men and slowly lowered the candle till it was almost touching Chas's cock. "Now?" he whispered.

"Yes. Please, oh please!"

The candle caressed the tip of his cock lightly. Once. Twice. It was as if the thing was on fire.

"Oh god!" Chas's come spurted out, covering the candle, staining his jeans, sliding off the man's dark fingers.

The man raised the candle to Chas's lips and made him lick off the glistening come, suck the thing clean. He thrust it deep into his throat, almost gagging him for a moment. Then he burst out laughing.

"You little tramp," he said. And he tossed the candle on Chas's naked crotch, got up swung into his coat. He was laughing as he shouldered his way out through the crowd.

Chas made a dive for his coat and covered his nakedness. But he wasn't sure if anyone had seen him or not. Hot with shame, he wriggled into his jeans and literally staggered out into the fresh air. He was still shaking.

When he was almost home, he stopped and looked at the candle he still held in his hand. "Shit," he muttered and slipped it back in his pocket.

Jack was watching skating on TV and eating corn chips and salsa.

"Check this out," Jack said, waving a chip at the screen. "It's that skater I told you about, the one I used to fuck in the parking lot behind the arena."

"No shit!" Chas glanced at the screen and gasped. The long black hair was pulled back into a pony tail but there was no disguising that face. Chas sank down onto the couch beside Jack. "I bet he was good, eh?" said Chas.

"You better believe it," said Jack.

Chas laughed and reached for a chip.

Chops

and the

stiff

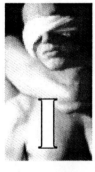

I was banging the kid's ass when I saw the body fall past my window. I live in a converted warehouse. The windows are big. The kid under me howled in ecstasy. I screamed. But I kept right on plowing him, riding faster and faster, as if spurred on by that glimpse of Andy 'The Handyman' Maquire falling to his doom. The kid was tied to the bed but he managed to get a lot of action going, slapping his ass against my nuts and howling like a banshee in heat. His arms were stretched wide, held tight by the handcuffs that rattled against the painted metal headboard. His muscles stood out rigid, like cables. His blond hair was slicked tight against his skull. His shoulders gleamed like slick marble in the light from the one naked light bulb swinging over the bed. Sometimes I like to read before going to sleep. A Walter Winchell column, maybe a story by that Parker doll. Or Damon Runyon's latest, just to see if I recognized anyone.

Tonight my bedtime story was a kid named Tony 'The Angel' Sanducci. He looked like a choirboy but the only singing he did was in a customer's bed. This time, he was doing a freebie, a thank you to me for taking him in on a slow night. Outside it was as cold as a witch's tit. I had spied him under his usual lamppost outside the YMCA as I walked home from my gig playing clarinet at The Pit, lugging my axe in my arms to keep warm. One look was all it took to get him trotting at my heels all the way home. So now the Angel was paying me back. In spades.

I came like Old Faithful on a really good day. I collapsed on the kid's muscular back, gasping and panting. I reached for a Lucky.

"You should lay off the nicotine and booze for a while, Chops," the Angel said.

"You should shut up." I smacked him on the ass. He grinned appreciatively. I thought of ambling over to the window to check on the status of Handy Maguire, my erstwhile upstairs neighbour, but I figured by now he was a goner so what was the point. My apartment is a walk-up but like I said, it's a converted warehouse with high ceilings. I'm on the fourth floor. The Handyman lived on the floor above me. Used to, that is. No way he was breathing. A police siren wailed in the night, coming closer. The Angel licked my ear. I forgot about the Handyman.

The next day, I was in the office suite I share with Cuddles LaJoya, the insurance investigator. To be more precise, I rent the broom closet she calls the second office at an exorbitant fee and we share a secretary, a little doll by the name of Hettie Gable. Her boyfriend made the whole deal worthwhile. Anyways, it was Friday and Hettie and the matinee idol had already jumped in the jalopy and headed out of town for the weekend. Cuddles had left early too, with her girl-friend, and I could still hear the shouting that passed for conversation between them all the way up the stair-well.

I was just thinking about maybe hitting the road myself when the door opened and Rudolph Valentino walked in. Actually, this citizen was a whole heap bet-ter looking than old Rudy ever was, except that his gorgeous velvet brown eyes were red and puffy and he looked like he'd lost his dog. Or maybe his best friend.

"I need help," he said.

Anything. I cleared my throat. "What seems to be the problem?" I leaned back on my squeaky chair and tucked my thumbs into my vest pockets.

"It's... my uncle." He folded all six feet of elegance into the chair opposite me and flung his brown fedora on my cluttered desk. He pulled a pack of Philip Morris out of his jacket pocket and lit up with a shaking hand. A diamond pinky ring caught the light and winked at me. I almost winked back.

I was smoking one of Cuddles' cigarillos. I flicked off the ash and waited for him to collect his thoughts. My own thoughts roamed over the elegant body hiding under the Savile Row suit. It was an effort to concentrate.

"My uncle died yesterday. The police say he... that he killed himself... jumped out of the window in his apartment on the fifth floor. They say—" He stopped and took a long drag on his cigarette.

I sat up abruptly and began to pay more attention. This citizen did not look like any relative of the Handyman. On the other hand, he wasn't paying me to think about family trees. On the third hand, he wasn't paying me. Yet.

"They say he left a note...."

"I'm very sorry for your loss," I said, "but I don't see what I can do for you."

"It wasn't suicide!"

"If he left a note, then I don't see how you can argue—"

"I don't care about the note! It's not possible, that's all." He stubbed out his cigarette fiercely, as if trying to annihilate the thing from the face of the earth. He was one unhappy citizen. And he had wonderful strong looking hands.

"Look, ah... I don't think I caught the name."

He raised his head and looked me square in the eye and I saw the thoughts roll through his head as plain as if he was talking out loud. He was going to lie. Then he changed his mind.

"I'm Richard Cunningham III," he said. "I can pay you handsomely."

"For what?"

"To find out what happened."

His eyes were a melting brown, (did I mention that?) and they were so deep I knew if I dived in I might never get out again. I didn't care. I'm a sucker for brown eyes. And besides, I need to eat, like the next guy.

"My name's D.D. Domingo, but my friends call me Chops."

"I know. You're a jazz musician part time. You play clarinet with the Dixie Cups at the Pit on Thursday nights."

"This is about Handy, isn't it?" I said "And he's not your uncle." Richard Cunningham III turned a lovely shade of magenta. I hurried on: "Don't worry, I'm the last person who'd try to shake you down. I knew Handy had someone, but he wouldn't talk. Made me wonder."

"Now you know."

Swell. Somehow the knowledge didn't make me feel any better about the whole thing.

"How about we mosey on over to Luigi's Diner on the corner and you can tell me what you think I can do for you," I said, reaching for my hat.

"Diner?" he said.

"The back room," I said. I winked. It was worth it just to see that wonderful blush creep up to the roots of his hair.

The back room at Luigi's was by invitation only. The tables there were far apart, with checkered cloths and candles for atmosphere and home made chianti flowing like water. The chef was a guy named Chris, wore a blond wig and lipstick and on special occasions, a dress. It took a while for Richard to relax, but when he did, his story flowed out of him all in one piece.

It seems our boy had been going with Andy for about a month. It was all very hush-hush, with Richard renting a suite at the Metropole under a false name and Andy sneaking in by a side entrance. I couldn't picture it myself, Richard not being the sneaking around type, know what I mean? Who can figure such things. So it turns out Richard had just talked Andy into letting him rent a classy pad in the village for the two of them where they could live as uncle and nephew.

I took another belt of vodka straight up and told him it didn't make no sense to me. Who could think about such things as suicide with a looker like this waiting for you at home? Not to mention paying the bills.

"He was going to keep his place in the warehouse to use as a workshop," he said, his voice wobbly. "He loved fixing things, you know? He was so creative that way." He pulled out his linen handkerchief and blew his nose. "He was worried about something, too."

"Like?"

He shrugged elegant shoulders. I poured him more wine. I remembered all those late nights, with Handy bumping up the stairs with yet another piece of old junk he found making his rounds in the wee small hours. He could fix anything, have it working good as new or better in a few hours, like as not. And he could refinish wood and patch up any old dresser or what not, sell it as a genuine antique down in the market. A real loss to society, in my books.

My companion had given up all pretense of the stiff

upper lip. He was bawling like a baby, what with too much wine and sympathy and all. There was no getting any more info out of him tonight. What could I do but take him home?

Apparently booze made the kid horny as hell. I was always horny so there was no problem there. We fell on each other right there on the couch, before we even got to the bed. I pulled off his trousers and pried him out of his boxers in no time at all. His equipment was as fine and elegant as the rest of him, none too long, perhaps, but pretty and anxious to please, rearing up straight from his belly and pointing at me. I gulped him down and suckled on him and drank his sweet milk like there was no tomorrow while he lay back, his dark head tumbled back off the couch, his hair hanging down in sweat-drenched locks as he bucked and moaned and carried on. When he came the second time he cried.

Then I flung him over on his stomach. He was limp as a rag doll, exhausted yet aching to be used as Andy had no doubt used him. I fucked his pretty pink dimpled ass. As I bucked and thumped into him, I glanced at the window and almost lost it. The light was just the same. I was pumping ass, just the same. My mind began playing tricks on me and I almost saw the Handyman's body fall past the glass, only this time in slow motion, giving me and him time to look at each other. My heart raced. I came.

I lay on the guy's back, catching my breath, my mind turning over like an eight cylinder engine going full speed ahead.

"Have you got a key?" I said at last.

He looked at me, his face tear stained. The brown eyes were luminous and sated. "Key?"

I jerked my head towards the ceiling. "Andy's place," I said.

He hiccuped a little and began to sit up and pull himself together. His face was pale, now, the sexual heat fading. "No. We always met at the Metropole. Why?"

"I want to take a look around up there. If it was a murder, we might find out the reason."

He looked about to lose it again so I pulled him into the shower and turned on the water full force. It took longer than usual to get clean, seeing as how I kept being turned on by the guy and he kept wanting to suck me off. Finally, the hot water gave out and so did we.

Dressed again, I armed myself with my trusty John Roscoe, my 'tool kit', a gift from a sexy second storey man of my acquaintance, and a flashlight and we started up the stairs. Half way up, the timed light went out, as per usual. Richard grabbed my arm. He was trembling. I flicked on the flashlight.

Andy had three locks on his door. He was funny that way. None of them was much of a challenge to me, though. As the door swung open, I caught Richard's hand reaching for the light.

"The cops might have a watch on this place outside," I hissed. "Cool it with the lights."

We went inside and closed the door behind us. Just like my place, there were no curtains on the windows.

The dull orange night of a big city that never sleeps seeped in, casting a strange pall over Andy's possessions. Like my place, too, the whole apartment was one open space. Junk was everywhere, piled in heaps, leaning against the walls, even hanging from the ceiling. Bicycles were chained to one wall. Wooden tea boxes were stacked against one another. In one corner, a workbench was set up, tools neatly lined up in place over a huge chest holding nails and different grades of sandpaper, small cans of refinishing stain and paint chips and bottles and rags. It was ordered chaos.

"It's hopeless," Richard said. "How can you find anything here?"

"It would help if I knew what I was looking for," I said. I ran my hand over a small table Andy had apparently been working on. The top was smooth as satin, There were two flaps that you could put up on either side to make the thing bigger and a small drawer in the middle. The drawer was missing.

"Looks like a desk over there." Richard went over to the window and started going through the drawers.

Junk, I thought. Junk that the Handyman turned into treasure. But was it valuable enough to kill for? Or had the kid who was going through his desk right now been telling the truth, the whole truth and nothing but the truth?

"Someone's coming!"

We got out of there like greased lightning, just as a couple of cops began thumping up the stairs. They paused to light up, giving us time to slip into my place. And out of our clothes.

The next morning, Richard was gone and there was an envelope with five C notes inside on my coffee table. Now I knew how the Angel must feel after a swell night with a client with bucks. Except Richard was supposed to be the client here, not me. I pocketed the C notes and decided not to think about it.

"We gotta stop meeting like this," I said to Cuddles LaJoya on the stairs outside our office.

"I'd be happy if we stopped meeting entirely," she snapped.

"Guess who hasn't had her java?" I said.

She grunted and disappeared into her office. "If you want some, come on in," she said over her shoulder. I did. "Take a load off," Cuddles went on, handing me a mug of steaming ink. Hettie had a way with coffee no one else had. Or wanted. Still, the stuff was useful to crank up the morning.

We chatted about this and that and then I told her about Richard III. I told her most of it, leaving out a few of the C notes, which was just as well because next thing I know she's holding out her hand and mentioning the tab I was running up for the rent. I handed over one of the notes, which seemed to satisfy her.

"So what do you know about lover boy?" she asked, getting down to detecting.

I guessed right off she didn't want to know about his dimpled ass, so I told her the stuff he'd told me about him and Andy.

"And you believe it?" she said, stabbing the air

with her cigarillo.

"Sure," I said. It sounded lame, even to me. Cuddles was pushing the wrong buttons so I picked up the java and made for my own broom closet, waving to Hettie en route.

By the afternoon I knew a lot more about Richard. I found out he'd been expelled from Princeton on some nebulous grounds. It didn't take a genius to figure that one out. Seemed he was always around this Reggie Harris, and they belonged to the same sailing club. When I phoned Richard to ask about Reggie he sputtered and stammered and I could just imagine the magenta blush rushing over his face.

"That was before I met Andy," he said at last. "And aren't you supposed to be investigating Andy's death, rather than snooping about in my business? That's what I'm paying you for, remember."

Properly reproved, I started dialing again. This time I found out Andy was a bit more of a horseplayer than I'd realized, but none of the bookies holding his markers were carrying all that much action. On the other hand, someone had recently bought up said markers. Someone big. Finally I found Mooch Munro in Kelly's Place and he whispered the name Lucky Mariano. It didn't make sense. I decided to go home and give the matter some serious thought.

Practically outside my building I ran into Tony 'the Angel' Sanducci, looking pinched and hungry. He had a black eye and a split lip.

"That door you walk into have a name?" I asked.

He shrugged. "Cost of doing business," he said.

That made me mad but there was nothing I could do about it. When I invited him inside for a little first aid and a drink, he didn't argue.

My place was looking pretty scruffy, too, what with the bed still unmade and dust lying thick on every surface. The Angel didn't seem to notice. He cleaned himself up and plopped down in my one armchair. Just about to put his feet on the coffee table, he stopped.

"Well, well. You're keeping some pretty dangerous company lately, I see, Chops." He was staring at Richard's calling card, that had been in the envelope with the C notes.

"A client," I said, "with killer eyes."

"And a killer boyfriend," the Angel said. I stared at him. "You don't know? That's Lucky Mariano's new boy, Rick The Gent."

I shook my head in astonishment at this news. It took the Angel a full five minutes to convince me, along with the information that Rick The Gent had picked up the Angel a week ago and pumped his ass, while the boyfriend pumped him for info about me.

"Well, I'll be damned," I said.

He agreed that I probably already was, considering the circumstances.

"He went to all that trouble just to get inside Andy's place? But why? They could have just broken in and trashed everything."

"Guess I gave the impression you two were more palsy then you were."

"Swell."

"Better we should check upstairs again," Tony suggested.

I nodded. I was remembering Richard's interest in Andy's desk and within minutes we were inside, checking through the papers it contained. Nothing.

Then my eye caught the table Andy had been working on, and the missing drawer. With something to look for, it took a mere twenty-five minutes to come up with it, inside a cabinet with a busted door.

"There's nothing there," the Angel pointed out.

Disappointed, we decided to give up, since we had no idea what we were searching for.

I invited the Angel to come with me to the club for some dinner and pick up my mail from Max. And found an envelope addressed to me in Andy's handwriting. Inside was a long flat key and a card with the words, "Stash this for me, please. I'll pick it up later. Thanks. Andy" scrawled on it.

"Weird looking key," the Angel remarked.

"It's for a safety deposit box. Come on. I gotta make some phone calls." I headed to my usual table.

It was pretty early for the guys who hang out at the Pit, but Max set us up with Reuben sandwiches and a plate of pickles and a telephone and left us alone. I called my favorite copper Teddy 'the Bear' Robinson and told him about the matter.

"We never bought that suicide note," Teddy growled. "Figured it was bad debts, though. This sounds more in'eresting."

"If you can be at The Pit around 11 tonight, I can guarantee you an interesting time," I said.

There was a pause. "As long as you're not playin',"

he said, and hung up.

Then I called Richard. It took some doing to talk him into it without mentioning the key, but I finally got him to agree to drop in around 11 tonight.

"This I gotta see," the Angel said. His eyes were so bright it sent shivers down my spine.

"If you're here, it'll blow the whole thing," I pointed out.

He pouted.

Then I told him about the small area backstage where the guys left their stuff before a gig. "You can watch from there," I said, "but stay out of sight."

By the time Richard arrived just after 11, the Angel was nowhere to be seen and the Bear was behind the bar with Max, cleaning glasses, with a stogie rammed in the corner of his mouth. Two other citizens who were probably cops sat sullenly at a table in one corner. A few more unhappy-looking customers held down another table by the bar. Apart from that, it was the usual crowd.

I showed Richard the envelope with the key and the sullen individuals by the bar were all over me. Richard changed before my eyes into Bugs Moran, heater and all.

"Get it, boys!" he said.

"You disappoint me," I managed, just before a fist slammed into my kisser.

It was all over by the time I came to. The Angel was leaning over me, holding my head in his lap and crying real tears.

"It's okay, kid," I assured him, rubbing my jaw. "Just

help me get back to my place."

"They took the Gent and a couple of Lucky's hoods down to the local slammer," the Angel told me. "The whole thing's to do with some extra set of books the Handyman found in that table he was fixing up."

"All he wanted to do was turn junk into antiques," I said, one arm around the kid's strong shoulders. "Guess he couldn't resist a little more larceny."

"Know what I can't resist?" The Angel smirked. "A good tool. Always turns me on. Especially when used by a good private dick."

Somehow, I was feeling better already as we lurched up the stairs to my place and tumbled in the door, heading for the bed.

This time I made sure I wasn't facing the damn window.

the

pick-up

It's late, about 4:30, I guess. I'm walking home from Jamie's place and I'm wasted. Hours of foreplay, heat and panting frustration. Hours spent watching the man dance for me, in nothing but a thong. Sometimes he'd disappear and then come back in a red dance belt or a leather jock. But he didn't want me to take off my jeans or even unzip them. He wanted me dressed, and writhing on the pillows of the huge couch while he postured and pranced, the golden light rippling up and down his muscles, his shaved legs and chest like living marble. I've waited so long to get this close to the guy I've watched on stage so often, only to watch him stroke himself to orgasm and come through the thin material of the dance belt. He did this several times and at last he ordered me to peel down my pants and jerk off in front of him. It took a long time. It was painful and strangely humiliating. Jamie seemed barely interested and wandered off to put on a silk gown leaving me gasping and shaking as I came all over my hands and his velvet cushion.

So now I'm stumbling through the pre-dawn haze, cutting through the parking lot behind my apartment building. I trip over something. At first I think it's wadded up paper, but something makes me look closer. It's a pair of Jockeys! The recognition sends a small jolt of sexual pleasure through me and I pick them up. I look around, feeling hot and jumpy, like I expect the guy who was wearing them to be watching me from behind a car or something. The briefs are dirty, as if a car ran over them but I wad them up and stuff them in the pocket of my jacket and get on home fast. I can't believe just picking up the thing is making me horny again!

When I close my apartment door behind me the first thing I do is take out the briefs and bury my face in them. I can smell the damp outdoors smell of early morning. I can smell a hint of gasoline and the grimy taste of dirt. I close my eyes and feel the thin cotton in my hands, run my fingers along the wide worn elastic, slide my thumb inside the pouch. Where his dick was. Slowly I bring the Jockeys close to my face and draw in my breath. Is it my imagination, or can I smell a tinge of urine?

My eyes fly open and I feel like a kid caught playing with himself. But I live alone. This is my apartment. I drop my jacket over the back of a chair, pull off my boots, pad down the hall to the bathroom. As I piss, I hold the Jockeys in my other hand, wipe my cock with them when I'm done. I peel off my t-shirt and jeans and stumble to my bed, still holding the briefs. I fall asleep inhaling the scent of my own piss and the vague sweat smell of a stranger.

Next day is Saturday and I have a lot of errands to run, boring things to do like shopping for food and dropping in to see my old man in the hospital. He's an okay guy but we never did talk much. We talk even less now, but I know he likes to see me now and then. Sometimes I gaze at him and wonder if I'll look like that when I'm his age. Will I have anyone coming to see me? Afterwards I go into a bar and drink five beers fast all in a row. Standing against the brick wall, I lean on my elbow and finally take the time to look around.

The afternoon sunlight shows the dust on the floor and tables and on the pictures of muscular guys on the walls. The few drinkers at the bar are older. There's a group of college age kids by the window, laughing and making fools of themselves. They don't interest me. I see what interests me standing alone in the shadows. He doesn't fit in here any more than I do. He's big, broad-shouldered, rough around the edges. He wears a Greek fisherman's cap pushed back on his thick grey-streaked curls. His boots are scuffed and lived in and so's the rest of him. When our eyes meet, they hold. I feel his interest, watch his mouth begin to smile. I wait until he crosses the room to my side.

"Come here often?" He smirks.

"Let's go."

"Fine by me." He ambles out the door letting me set the pace. I'm suddenly in a hurry to get him back to my place. We start to walk briskly. In the bright light outside, he looks even better. He's not as tall as me but he's stocky and strong. I can picture me riding his back. I feel the sweat break out on my forehead.

"Warm, isn't it?" he says. His eyes twinkle.

"I live here," I say. I don't want to get to know to him. He's my fantasy man. I know what I want him to do and it isn't talk.

Upstairs on the fifth floor, we go inside and I pull the drapes, keeping out the sun. It's a studio apartment and my bed fills half of it. He takes off his boots and pulls off his t-shirt.

"Nice place," he says.

I'm holding the old soiled briefs in both hands, balled up. I knead them nervously, wondering how he'll respond to what I want him to do.

"I want you naked," I say, my eyes glued to his broad thighs and solid ass. What's between his legs doesn't interest me so much.

He shrugs and begins to take off his clothes, dropping them on the chair beside the table. I think he's enjoying this, being told what to do, not having to talk. His body emerges into the dimmed light of the room, sturdy and strong, softly furred on his chest and arms and legs. His dick is short and thick. As he turns, I see a tattoo on his shaved ass. The tattoo is old but it looks like an eagle with a heart in its beak.

I can feel my heart begin to trip faster as I undress,

too. I leave on my black bikini briefs as I turn to face
him. He's waiting, head cocked as he scratches his furry
chest.

I pick up the Jockeys and hand them to him. "Put
these on."

He frowns, puzzled, and takes the underwear in his
hands. He holds them out, studying the thin cotton,
the worn elastic and stretched pouch. "A trophy?" he
asks.

"Something like that." I'm getting anxious now,
afraid he may object to putting on unwashed dirty
underwear. I realize suddenly that without the Jockeys,
I don't want the man. I watch, my eyes narrowed,
almost holding my breath.

"This is important to you."

I nod.

He shrugs and begins to put on the briefs, leaning
against the wall to steady himself. I flash back to when
I was a kid, standing outside in the flower bed watching my Uncle Leo through the bedroom window. He
was younger than my father, played football for his college team. He was blond but he had the same thick
thighs as this guy, the same deliberate way of shoving
his feet through the leg holes of his BVDs. I snap my
mind back to the present.

"They fit," says my visitor. He struts over to the
window, back to the wall. He looks good and he knows
it. "So, are we going to do anything or is this just a
fashion parade of faded glories?" He tugs at his own right
nipple and I feel an instant response.

I remember my frustration with Jamie last night

and move in close at once. I can feel the heat from his body even before I touch him. My fingers wander over his chest, down the soft mound of his belly where his waist spreads comfortably under the old elastic of the briefs. He lets out his breath in a sigh and leans back against the wall, letting me explore him.

Slowly I sink to my knees. My eyes are on a level with his crotch, now. The tracks from the tire spread across the filling pouch like skid marks. Already the man's cock is straining the cotton, pushing out the soiled pouch. I can see it through the slit, dark, throbbing with desire. I put my face right against the briefs, breathing in his musk through the material. Closing my eyes, I conjure up the man who bought these briefs, big and handsome and generous with his body. As I press my mouth against the warm cotton, it's as if I'm going down on two men, the sturdy man from the bar and that other shadow-man who's memory still lingers around his discarded underwear.

My tongue slides inside the slit, touching the pulsing smoothness of my companion's cock. He catches his breath and one big hand drops onto my hair. I shake him off. I want to do this completely on my own, allow my fantasies to roam over both the men who quiver and moan at the touch of my tongue.

The front of the briefs is soaked with my saliva and my mouth is full of the mingled taste of sweat, urine, and the gritty crust of the parking lot. Under the touch of my hands, his massive thighs shudder. He moans and pushes his legs farther apart.

I slide one finger through the leg hole on the right.

His cock jumps and I can feel his hairy balls. My own cock swells painfully, pushing against the black nylon of my bikinis. I pull down the thin black strip, releasing my cock. My other hand snakes between his legs, my finger pushing up into the secret heat of his body. He grunts in pleasure.

"Yeah," he growls, twisting himself against my hand.

But the angle is wrong. The leg band restricts any further penetration and I withdraw my hand, put my fingers to my lips and sniff the smell of his ass.

The man moves then, turning towards my only arm chair for support, leaning against it with his back to me. It's clear what he wants, what I want. I push his head down towards the cushions. His broad hairy back curves in submission. His ass is all mine.

Still on my knees, I gaze at the place where the thin cotton is almost translucent across his crack. I can see a faint outline of his tattoo. Saliva gathers as I lean forward and open my mouth, wetting the material until it gives way beneath the sudden thrust of my tongue. My mouth is invaded with the taste of him, tangy and sour. For a moment the taste of both my shadow man and my companion mingle in my mouth. Then my tongue pushes up into his crack, finds the tight rosebud of his ass and slowly forces it to open.

I can hold back no longer. I struggle up and push my bursting cock through the ragged hole I made. He reaches back with both hands, catching each cheek of his ass, opening himself up for me as I thrust inside. The velvet heat of him sucks me in deeper, deeper. We are joined at one spot, yet still separated by the worn grey-tinged cotton of a stranger's briefs.

We are grunting and moaning almost in unison, now. I can feel the pressure build and I am not able to hold back. I come and collapse against his wide back. A moment later he comes, without even touching himself. We both slide to the floor.

"Fuckin' A," he says. He's grinning. The front of the old Jockeys is slick with come.

I grin and wipe myself off with my black bikinis. I remind myself to get the Jockeys back before he leaves. I am already thinking of the next time, of the third man who will wear them.

the

provider

"I'm not a pimp!" cried Bryce. "I'm a provider. A care-giver."

"You're trying to make me dependent on you!" Galen shouted. "I need the taste of the streets!"

"They're trash, can't you see? They sell themselves for a fix!"

"And you don't? Who are you that you should presume to judge!"

"I'm only trying to save you from kids like Zane."

"Be silent!" Galen's voice exploded against the shadowed walls. The tall narrow windows shook behind the velvet drapes.

Bryce stood his ground. He had seen the mindless anger, the searing rage, many times. He knew what it meant. "I have kept you from becoming an animal," he said softly.

Galen smiled, in control again. "So you like to think. If it gives you pleasure, go ahead."

Pleasure. The word, spoken by Galen's pale blood-starved lips seemed stripped of meaning, an empty word with no associations.

Galen slumped back in the ornate chair, a pale hand curved over each armrest. The blast of anger had drained him. His head was bent, the soft blond hair falling over his forehead. The nape of his neck gleamed ivory in the dim light.

Bryce knew this creature was incapable of love, but the knowledge made no difference. His fanatical devotion burned strong and hot as ever. At times, he knew that Galen hated him. At times when he was needed. Like now. But Bryce still clung to one fact. Galen needed him. And every now and then, he would have to acknowledge this.

Galen raised his head and stared across the dim room, lit by the soft oil lamps he insisted on. His green eyes glowed dully. His face looked gaunt, the pallid skin stretched tight over the high cheek bones. Bryce looked away. He couldn't stand to see the one he loved suffer, but he must. It was all he had.

"Come closer, Bryce. I'm weak. You know when I'm weak." The voice was a whisper on the air, more like a subtle suggestion than words. "How can you turn away from me now? You know what to do."

Bryce nodded. Even after the fights, his pain, he knew he would open his shirt and kneel in front of

Galen, between his long legs. Because only then, while Galen sucked his life blood from the plastic tube inserted over his heart, would he allow Bryce to touch him.

Bryce opened his shirt and knelt. He gathered Galen into his arms, guiding the pale head to his chest. He winced as he felt the hot dry lips touch his skin, felt the first strong pull. For a moment, he swayed and had to steady himself. Then his hand went to Galen's bent head, his fingers straying through the fine spun-gold hair. He could almost feel the strengthening pulse at the temples, under his finger tips. Because of me, he thought. I am his life. But his elation was brief. He knew anyone could perform this task. Others had before him. If he wasn't careful, others would again. He bent his head and touched the silky hair with his lips.

With a shuddering sigh, Galen pulled away, as always forcing himself to stop well before he had slaked his thirst. He laid his head back against the carved oak. Waiting. Allowing Bryce his one act of intimacy.

Bryce slid to the floor. As he undid the buttoned fly, he forced all thoughts out of his head. He, too, was hungry, with a thirst that would never be satisfied. The damp earthy smell made his senses reel as he opened his mouth to his lover's cool white flesh.

All too soon, it was over.

"We're little better than cannibals," Galen said with a lazy smile. He wiped a trickle of blood from the corner of his mouth with one finger. "We feed off each other."

"You are surprisingly whimsical sometimes," remarked Bryce, buttoning up his shirt. As always, he felt slightly sick after submitting to Galen. It was a delayed reaction, that hit when he stood up. He made his way carefully to the table and helped himself to wine.

Galen stretched, lifting his arms to the ceiling, arching his back, twisting slightly at the hips with sensual grace. Already colour had seeped back into his cheeks, staining the fine skin like crushed strawberries. The green eyes sparkled, a fire that gave no heat. "Get your jacket. It's time for you to go out."

"I told you— Go yourself. You don't need me."

"I know." Galen was enjoying himself. It was as if the shouting and the intimacy had never taken place. They both knew that Bryce was powerless, now, helpless to stop what would happen next.

"Galen, I'm not going."

"Aren't you my 'provider'? My 'care-giver'? You said so yourself just a few minutes ago." He smiled, the green eyes taunting, cold as ice, slicing into his soul.

Bryce sighed. "How many?"

"Three would be nice. See what you can do." Galen turned away, his mind already moving on to the designs he would sketch for the eighteenth century movie that was his current project. It amused him to reproduce on stage the clothes he and his friends had worn in the long vanished days of his youth. It amused him still more when he was praised for the historical accuracy of his designs.

Bryce watched him leave the room, listened to his

light step going up the stairs. He glanced at his watch. All the strength and purpose seemed to have drained out of him. From far off in the bay, the low wail of the fog horn echoed his despair.

Outside, the cool dampness of the evening kissed his lips with salt. Long ribbons of mist swirled along the driveway, hiding the low bushes and setting the trees adrift in a sea of fog. The sickly yellow glow of the wrought iron gas lamps made little impact on the gloom. Bryce shivered as he got into the car.

When the gates of the estate slid shut behind him, Bryce slipped a cassette in the tape deck, hoping the music would soothe him. After a few moments, he switched it off. I hate him, he thought, giving the wheel a savage twist to the right. The big car spun out briefly, then straightened. Rain spat at the windshield.

Bryce took a deep breath and headed downtown.

He was always surprised by how easy it was to pick up boys. He had never had the desire to do so for himself, and the first time he had come here for Galen had been difficult for him. But merely a mention of Galen's connection with the movies was enough to gain the interest of the most half-hearted hustler. They were all eager to win his favour. They never could, of course. Except for one. Bryce winced at the memory, the tall, wide-eyed boy with the black hair curling down his back. Zane, a name as false as the angelic smile.

The fog was thicker near the water. The great black car slid through the deserted streets, gliding slowly through the swirling mist. Tonight's hunt took longer than usual, but at last he found two. They were friends, apparently. Once the fee was settled on, Bryce discouraged conversation. He preferred to keep his distance.

When they got back to the house, he found the studio empty. Bryce led the boys down the hall to the master bedroom and knocked.

Galen flung open the door, a brocade robe draped carelessly over his slender body. He was naked underneath. "You took too long," he said. His green eyes glowed in the dimness. Over his shoulder, Bryce glimpsed the four poster bed, a familiar tousled head, a long pale thigh. "I've made my own arrangements. Get rid of them."

Bryce thrust his foot in the space between the door and the jamb. "You promised— You swore to me you wouldn't go out. We had an agreement!"

Galen laughed. "You are a fool," he said. "You think you can contain me, my appetites, my needs? I am far beyond your feeble comprehension." He began to press the door against Bryce's foot, a steady pressure, without apparent effort on his part. "How do you think I have survived as long as I have?"

Bryce winced as the bones in his foot began to grind. Tears came to his eyes but he refused to acknowledge the pain, to back down before that pent up malevolence. "I'm not afraid of you," he said, his voice shaking. "Do what you want. Kill me! Would that make you happy?"

"Happy? You are a bigger fool than I realized!" Galen gave the door a final excruciating squeeze.

In spite of himself, Bryce cried out in pain. "Damn you, Galen!"

"I was damned a long time ago, and you had nothing to do with it!" Galen released the pressure, kicked the mangled foot away. "Run the bath for me." He slammed the door in Bryce's face.

Bryce leaned against the wall trying to control his ragged breathing. The boys had disappeared. He could hear their steps pounding down the stairs and across the hall. The front door opened. Closed. He was alone. Except for Galen. And Zane.

He wiped his face with his sleeve. "It's over," he whispered. But how can something be over which never really began? It was all a fantasy, spun out of his own heated imagination. He had tried, oh how he had tried to make Galen desire him, need him. How he had tried to open his veins to that hot mouth and be drained to the point of floating between their two worlds. Only by doing this could he join Galen forever, be at his side, his shadow, his lover.

But Galen had always refused, forcing himself to back off time and again, keeping Bryce at a distance by inserting the tube over his heart, so they would barely touch as he fed. Over and over Bryce had brought home boys, young men, anyone whose eyes were needy, whose lips would ask no questions, whose bodies would not be missed if Galen became violent, as he did sometimes. Especially if there was no one there to stop him.

Slowly Bryce dragged himself along the hall to the huge old fashioned bathroom. He would obey once more. But this time, there would be a difference.

He ran water into the bathtub, mounted on its graceful clawed feet. He threw in handfuls of scented beads. It was agony taking the shoe off his mangled foot. Blood oozed from the crushed toes as he peeled back the sock. He had to keep stopping, letting the pain roll over him. At last, he gently lowered himself into the warm water. He wondered idly if Galen had always been a sadist or if this had come on him centuries ago, with the Change.

The warmth was calming. The scented oils wreathed the room in heady perfume. The throbbing of his foot was almost pleasurable, now. He reached out for the ivory handled straight razor on the shelf behind him. Without pausing, he drew the thin bade across first one wrist, then the other. He watched, fascinated as his blood swirled slowly into the water. Then he grasped the tube above his heart and pulled. The unexpected pain jolted him, and for a moment he was afraid. Then the warmth swam over him again and he closed his eyes.

When he heard the door click, he opened them again. Galen was kneeling beside him, a silver goblet in one hand. The green eyes burned so brightly, Bryce blinked in pain.

"Fool," Galen remarked. He reached down and pulled the plug to let out the reddened water. "Never waste good blood." He pressed the silver goblet against Bryce's chest and watched blood ooze over the rim.

Bryce smiled as Galen's fingers touched his chest, squeezing the artery to pump the blood out faster. Then the smile faded as he became aware of another person in the room. Zane. Naked. He was very pale. Several scars stood out against the whiteness of his neck.

"Come," murmured Galen, holding out his goblet to the boy. "Drink. A token of my love."

The last clear image that Bryce's mind recorded was the picture of Zane's full lips, blood red against the silver.

watching

I t looks warm and dark and inviting in the alley behind his apartment house. I am walking back from the parking lot, cutting through from the street along the lane that services the building where Partners Bar is. I can still hear the croon of the guitars and the wail of a man singing. I jump down from the cement divider, into the shadows. There is no wind here. My boots make only a dull thud, the sound cushioned by layers of damp leaves and someone's old mattress. I pause a moment to get my bearings.

It is the secret hidden world behind those golden windows that draws me. I have always been fascinated by the lives of strangers, how people change when they shed their outer skins at their own front door and slip into something more comfortable, more themselves. I do it myself. But even if you go with them, follow them home through the night, follow them into that small stale apartment with the old socks in the corner and the bed unmade since this morning, you never catch them, never see the change first hand. At best you have efficient, hurried sex, after a desultory conversation. At worst, the stranger seen against his intimate background is no longer anonymous enough to satisfy. But glimpsed through the window, moving uninhibited though his own clear space, he becomes unattainable, an object of infinite conjecture. Desire twists inside me and the barrier of glass turns the scene into magic.

I hunch forward into my denim jacket, hands in pockets, and glance over my shoulder. Separated pools of light etch deeper shadows against the chain link fence and the corners around the loading dock. Nothing stirs. The soft night air touches my face, my neck, riffling against the exposed skin of my throat like a careless hand and leading me on. Head down, I move along the wall, sure of my way even though the night presses close here, hiding all detail. I keep to the edge of the alley, instinctively treading where the leaves cushion my footsteps.

At the gap between the buildings, I turn and plunge without hesitation into the narrow space. Above me, the buildings lean towards each other in conspiring darkness. With a soft grunt of exertion, I swing up to the grill that covers the deep well of the heating system. It is warm, here, the dampness of the decaying leaves strong on the air. I put one foot against the wall behind me and lean back, prepared to wait. However long it takes this time. Like always. My head is at just the right angle. For a moment, I feel a stab of panic, a quick falling away in the pit of my stomach. Perhaps I am too early. Perhaps he has decided to spend the evening with friends. Above me, I can hear the sound of a radio, the heavy beat of the bass line throbbing. The window lights up. I see him.

I take a deep, careful breath. It's like inhaling the essence of what is outside, and what I see in that room behind the glass. I draw it down into my lungs and from there it moves into my blood and the man I watch becomes a part of me. His straight fall of black hair. His intense dark eyes. The small cleft in his chin. The long mouth that crooks up slightly at one corner. He throws his leather jacket over the back of a chair, drops a magazine on the coffee table. He moves through the room, loose-limbed inside his clothes. I lick my lips, tasting the night and the sharp edge of my own longing.

A scrabbling in the dry leaves startles me, as a cat runs by the alley. For a moment, I lose the thread, my mind shying away from the man safe in the room in front of me, snagged by a moving shape in the shadows. Then it is gone. My eyes refocus, as the man stretches his arms above his head, pulling off his t-shirt. The light from the lamp by the tape deck highlights his cheekbones and the curve and dip of the muscles of his shoulders as they emerge from the shirt. Soundless in the circle of golden light, he stands and looks at his reflection in the mirror, a reflection I can just see if I tilt my head to the left. It is an image twice removed from me, a fainter likeness, a picture that is closer to memory than reality. If I lean across the damp air and touch the glass of his window, I cannot touch the man, or his image, and the gap between us widens in my mind, even as my longing for this touch jolts through me with despair. In the darkness, I fumble with the snap at the front of my jeans.

On the other side of the glass, my icon begins to study his reflection, moving his hand slowly over the expanse of his broad chest as if discovering himself. His fingers rake though the swirl of black hair between his dark nipples, move lower, pausing over his ribs. He breaths in. His ribs stand out, each bone curving sharp and precise under the skin. His belly sucked in, leaves a slight space between the silver buckle of his jeans and his concave stomach. He bends his head and the black hair falls over his eyes. I hold my breath, waiting, watching as he glances up again at his reflection, as if trying to catch himself off guard. It almost makes me laugh, except that for an instant, I see his eyes and they are deep with fear. My own hand falters, and I shrink against the wall, feeling like a child caught spying and about to be punished. But the moment passes, and when I look again, his eyes are flat and self-absorbed, his hands against his back, holding his body like a chalice, studying the effect.

My own body relaxes and the warmth grows inside me as I watch. He moves away from the mirror, his arms swinging, now, shoulders lifting to untie the knotted tension between his shoulder-blades. As my hand moves deeper, my fingers curling around my own hardening flesh, my eyes drink in the lean figure above me, every detail sharp as he loosens his jeans and they drop without sound to the floor. He stands unmoving, the jeans, shapeless pools around his ankles, the lean flanks dark, bronzed by the yellow light. I can feel the air against my naked skin as my own jeans hang open and am touched by the darkness and the cold hand of night. I shiver, but the sensation of vulnerability brings with it the heightened thrill of possible discovery, sharpening my senses, arousing me at last, as the connection between me and the almost naked young man inside tightens, twists, builds to a crescendo within me. I brace myself against the brick wall. My hand moves faster. He turns towards the window. I close my eyes, almost as if I think by not seeing him he can not see me, but when I open them again, he has turned away and is walking, slim-hipped and now completely naked, towards the door. He pauses, bends over, picks up his jeans. I smother my cry as I see the soft insides of his thighs, the secret darkness between his cheeks, open for a few seconds to my hot gaze. My knees are weak and my head arches back against the unfeeling brick. My breath is fast, coming in ragged gasps.

It is over.

Inside, the young man has turned off one of the lights. In partial shadow, he walks away from me, armed again in impenetrable mystery.

Outside, in the darkness, I bend my head and do up my jeans. The air is cool. Damp. There is moisture on my cheek. I walk out of the alley, narrowly missing the garbage cans set out by the corner of the building. I walk the streets, aimless, watchful. Seeing everything and nothing. At last I go home.

"How are things at the bar?" Evan asks, as he always does. He's wearing his dressing gown, old and barely decent, but it comforts him. I know this and try not to comment.

"Same as usual," I say. I pick up his leather jacket from where he always leaves it over the back of the chair and hang it up with mine.

"If it's always the same, why do you bother?" he asks.

"Perhaps because it *is* always the same," I say, more to annoy him than anything else.

He surprises me. He smiles, his long generous mouth crooking up on one side, his dark eyes laughing at me. "Touching," he says.

I flush. My jaw tightens. I can feel the anger, but I refuse to give in to it. "Sure," I say. "I'm going to bed."

"Want a smoke first?" Those black eyes hold me, skewered, squirming.

I hesitate, wondering what he knows, what he feels, if he still wants anything from me. I shake my head. "I gave it up, remember?"

He shrugs and picks up his book. His black hair is damp from the shower. Long tendrils curl against the soft vulnerability of his neck.

I watch him for a moment in the mirror. I can see him there as the boy he used to be, the young man he is now, and the spectre of what he will become, and my chest tightens painfully. I lay my hand against the glass, against the reflection of his bowed head, waiting till the hard surface absorbs my heat.

"You'll leave a smudge," he says.

I feel words, like knives, in my mouth. I don't let them out. Instead, I pick up the belt with the silver buckle and take it into the bedroom.

hot stuff

Want to know what turns me on? I'm walking down a crowded street and some guy bumps into me and I smell that heady mixture of sweat and hot skin and a bit of leather from the jacket he's wearing and I feel that rush. You know what I mean? I want to take that guy into the alley and pull down his pants and bend him over and fuck his bare ass right there in the hot afternoon sun! I don't want to know his name or what he likes to drink or whether he listens to opera— Hell, I don't give a fuck! I just want to hear him grunt and feel that furry ass under my hands as I pump into him. I can smell my own come dripping out of him. I can see the worn Levi's crumpled around his ankles, hobbling him so he can't move in those worn boots of his. He wears Jockeys and they're a little stained. While he's still bending over, his cock jerking in his hand, his ass-cheeks shaking, the print of my fingers still outlined in his pale flesh where I gripped his waist, I take my knife out of its sheath and cut off his underwear and put it in my pocket. I slap his ass once, watching the skin blush. Then I turn and walk away. Neither one of us ever says a word. That turns me on.

Or maybe it's a sassy drag queen parading down the street in the evening, long muscular legs silken smooth in black nylon, patent pumps with high fuck-me heels, and an ass that gets me so hot just looking at it I start to shake. Oh, yes. But she's a lady and I know she won't stand for me dragging her into a filthy alley. No way. So I buy her a drink and watch her long fingers play with the string of pearls around her neck and listen to that breathy voice. I wonder how long her cock is...where her cock is...when I can see it.

"Do you have a light?" she says.

Gawd, it's Marlene Dietrich. I'm getting hot for Marlene Dietrich.

"Come on," I say. "I've got a fucking torch at my place."

So we get there and I start to take off my shirt.

"Have you got any candles?" she says, looking around. She walks across my living room like she's on a runway, or something. That ass, high and round. Muscular. Gawd!

So I find some old white candles and I light them. I wonder if I'm going to have to redecorate the whole fucking apartment before I see some skin. I watch her deep brown eyes grow large and lustrous in the golden light and at last she begins to take off her clothes and I see small cinnamon tits emerge and I lick them and suck them and chew on them. We go to bed. Those large fluttering hands are suddenly strong and sinewy. I feel them kneading my ass, parting my cheeks and in she plows with that invisible dick.

Yes! Yessss!

I shout, clench my hands, arching my back. Her perfume is all around me. I come. The sheet sticks to my stomach as I buck, my asshole clutching that dick I've never seen. It's weird, but this, too, is hot.

But sometimes it's hot just to lie together and feel your furry chest and the thump, thump of your heart. Like now, stud.

Just like now....

aquamarine

-a fairy tale

Far out in the middle of the sea, the water is as blue as cornflowers, as clear as glass, and deeper than any anchor of any ship afloat. Down there beyond the reach of men live the water people, who are neither male nor female, human nor fish, but a wonderful combination of all four. Their country is full of beautiful plants and flowers and the sun floats down in bars of shimmering gold. All manner of amazing creatures live there, too. They glow every colour of the rainbow and a lot more besides that we have no words for.

At the bottom of the ocean, way down so deep that many steeples one on top of the other would never reach, stands the coral castle of the Sovereign of the Sea. It rises in graceful spires and turrets, twisting up through the water in elegant arabesques. Bright winged fish swoop past the arched windows, just as birds do here, and dazzling flowers and luminous waving grasses adorn its crevices and tiny balconies.

The Sovereign of the Sea lived here with his five children and many adoring servants. The King's mate was long gone, dissolving in a spray of bright foam on the top of the waves one evening as the sun sank slowly into the sea, until all signs vanished forever. But they were a happy family nonetheless, the children roaming about their beautiful palace, finding delight in small and unexpected things. As the years passed, they wandered further and further, discovering new and dazzling objects to marvel at.

They had all heard tales of the land of men, but none of them had seen it yet, as they were not allowed to break the surface of the water until their eighteenth birthday. They all longed to visit this mysterious place, but none with such intense yearning as the youngest.

Clare was named for the brightness of his shining hair and for his beautiful voice. He was the most handsome of the children, with a perfect mouth and great sparkling green eyes. He loved the silken ripple of the water against his body as he wove slowly through the coral arches of the palace, his hair mingling with the sea grasses, pulling gently against his scalp. Every pore of his pale skin drank in the sensations and little ripples of pleasure ran through his young lithe body. Since he was of the royal clan, as he grew older he decorated his tail with pearlized clam shells, shivering with delight as the objects pinched hard against his brilliant scales. "We cannot have both style and comfort," his father said, touching the decorations gently and smiling his calm smile. Clare didn't tell him that he enjoyed the pain. It was his and his alone. He had no words to express it. It touched something deep and dark inside, which he was too young to analyse. It reminded him of the leisurely times he lay among the mosses in the palace garden, exploring his own body, which was gradually changing, maturing, becoming something 'other' and inexplicably exciting. Pale hair now sprouted like corn silk where his scales grew larger and softer below his narrow waist. His small nipples pushed outwards, surrounded by an aureole of dark honey. He touched himself with languid hands, feeling the change in texture of his body as he ran his hands over the scales, through the silken hair and into the pale taut skin of his chest. He touched the hard nipples and shivered again and smiled. He wondered if his siblings enjoyed this, but he was suddenly too shy to ask them. At times he spied on them as they lay about in the long languorous afternoons, and once he found his older two siblings entwined in an upside down embrace. He felt hot and excited and glided to his own bower to run the picture through his head over and over as he undulated against the lichen-draped walls. But it was all like a fragile unfocused dream to him, until he found the statue.

It sometimes happened that things drifted down from the ships of men that rode atop their watery realm. In their wanderings, the youngsters had found all manner of things, but usually these objects were disguised by the sea to such an extent that it was impossible to discover their true meaning. The statue came floating down one morning, as Clare was in the part of the garden that he had claimed for his own. The sea youth opened his arms and the white marble statue drifted close and stared at him with wide open stone eyes. The statue was about as tall as Clare, but had no scales and no long tail. Instead, it stood on two sturdy muscular legs.

"What can it be?" Clare asked his tutor, who happened to be there, half asleep on the mossy couch.

"It is the likeness of a young male, a human man," the tutor replied, combing his beard thoughtfully.

Clare let his breath out in a long sigh and knew at last what he had been longing for. "I want to be a man," he said, but his tutor had fallen asleep again, which was probably just as well. He would merely say what was plainly evident: Clare was a sea prince. He would never be a man.

After this, Clare took the statue to his chamber and lay cradled against the smooth hard body, dreaming of life in the open spaces above the waves. He was fascinated with the shape and feel of the lower torso. His hands roamed over the unfamiliar contours of the male thighs and lingered in the space between the legs, fondling the odd external organ he found there. He yearned to reach his eighteenth birthday.

One by one his siblings attained the magic age of ascent and rose up through the waves to view the world of men for the first time. They came back with wondrous tales of ships and storms that sang thunderous music, of shining sandy beaches and green trees and a shade of blue that they had never seen before arching above their heads. But they had never ventured very close to the land and had always watched the men they found from a very safe distance. Although there was no longer any restriction on their surfacing, they quickly wearied of the novelty. Clare vowed to be much more venturesome when it was finally his turn.

At last the long-awaited day arrived. His family gathered around him and his tutor gave a lengthy explanation of what he should look for and when he should return. His old nurse helped twine a rope of pearls around his neck. His flashing tail was decorated with eight clam shells and his long pale hair was held back with a wide band of coral.

"Happy birthday, my dear," said his father, and he kissed his youngest on the forehead. They all rose through the water together, swirling around him in a murmuring chorus of encouragement. The water grew lighter, turning from deep green to light green, to blue.... Sunshine spilled over him in floods of gold. With a great cry of exhilaration, his head broke the surface and salt spray danced around him in the bright air. He was in the land of men!

At first he was so overwhelmed he could make out next to nothing. His sparkling green eyes darted about, eager to drink it all in. So much brightness! Such heady colours! And the sounds were beyond anything he had ever heard before. Birds called to each other as they swooped above him in the bowl of brilliant blue that was the sky. The waves pitched about, splashing around him playfully. The wind sang and tossed his hair like the fine spray of the foam. He was out of breath from sheer excitement as he danced on his strong muscular tail on the undulating sea.

He remembered the stories his siblings had told of rocks and beaches and ships, and he swam close to land, close enough to see the sparkling white sand and the vivid green of the trees that crowded close to the water. He filled his eyes with the beauty of the scene, the long lazy curl of water breaking in lace along the crescent curve of the beach. Red-roofed houses clustered in tiers above it and to one side rose a breath-taking palace, whose turrets gleamed white and gold in the sunshine.

He swam on and on, dancing and leaping further and further, past a great sparkling iceberg and beyond that, far in the distance, a range of snow capped mountains. But the winds here were cold and he soon headed back south, swimming swiftly with the current back to warmer climes.

And then he saw the boat. Even before he saw it, he could hear the men laughing and talking on board and heard the gentle complaint of the ropes and the sighing of the canvas sails. By now, clouds were scudding across the sun and the water had turned a silvery pewter colour. The boat rocked and heeled as the wind stiffened, racing through the rigging. One of the men had climbed onto the spit of wood that stuck far out in front of the ship and stood with legs apart, his black hair streaming behind in the wind. Clare knew he must be a prince of royal blood, for he was dressed in a rich red velvet jacket and tight fitting silken hose outlined the muscular curves of his legs. Just like the statue, Clare thought, and he could almost feel those legs and the bulge he saw between them. He felt a sudden sharp ache in his heart and he longed to touch the man, so alive, so full of laughter and the sense of adventure. The others were begging him to come back and at last, he leaped down onto the deck, reassuring them that all was fine, and they continued to feast and play music and talk as the sun disappeared behind the clouds and the wind built to a gale force.

The storm was wild. Clare raced to keep up, not wanting to lose track of the ship and its precious cargo. At first he laughed with the excitement of the chase, but then he realized the sailors were full of fear. Lightning split the sky and thunder crashed around them. The main mast of the ship snapped, sending a score of sailors with it over the side. Clare was just in time to see the prince swept overboard as a huge wave washed the deck clean. Catching the young man in his arms, Clare leapt away towards the shore, remembering to keep the man's head above water at all times. Before long, they came to the crescent shaped beach he had glimpsed earlier that morning and he realized, from what he had overheard, that this must be where the prince was from. Nearby, he saw the domes of the palace outlined in tiny lights. Every window was filled with the soft glow of candles.

Clare carefully laid the priceless burden on the fine white sand, taking the time to push the long black hair away from the pale face. The Prince's eyes were closed, but his broad chest still rose and fell. Clare kissed the pale lips, breathing new life into the man with all his might, and then slipped back into the water to wait.

All night he kept watch from a rock in the middle of the small inlet, until at last he saw a young girl walking along the beach. She knelt down beside the prince and touched his face and he awakened. Clare stayed just long enough to see them talking together, then fled back to his palace under the sea to dream about the black-haired prince from the world above the water.

Clare could no longer find happiness in his old life. He didn't want to go above the waves either, since what he saw would only intensify his longing to join the world of men. He lost all interest in everything. He still slept with his beloved statue in his arms, but now when he looked at it, he saw it was a lifeless thing, a pale reflection only of the prince it so resembled.

At last he could bear it no longer and he made his way to the cave of Orcane the Sorcerer. It was a frightening place, glowing with an unholy green phosphorescence and guarded by a coven of writhing serpents. Orcane himself wore two small sea serpents in his hair and when he spoke, red bubbles issued from his mouth along with the words.

"What you wish will bring nothing but heartache," he said, before Clare had even opened his mouth.

"But.... I already have heartache," he whispered.

"What you feel now is nothing compared to what you will go through in the land of men."

"I wish to be one of them," Clare said, his voice stronger. "I wish to be a man."

The sorcerer laughed. Billows of red stained the water of the cave and a rumbling echo prolonged the noise. Clare started back in fright, but soon regained his composure. His determination grew even stronger.

"And will you give me something in return?" the old sorcerer asked.

"Whatever you wish."

"I wish to take all your pretty words, and all the songs you will ever sing. Do you agree?"

Clare swallowed. "If this will make me a man, yes. I agree."

"And you will walk upright on two legs. But every step will cause you great pain. Do you still agree?"

"Yes, I agree."

"You are a fool." The sorcerer reached into his hair and withdrew one of the serpents and whispered to it. For a few minutes, a red cloud enveloped them and then the sorcerer's hand thrust the writhing snake at Clare.

He was frightened, but he forced himself to let the serpent slither around his chest. He shuddered as its muscular body undulated lower, lower, squeezing and rubbing against his sensitive scales in a way that made Clare blush. He thought of the black-haired prince and the blush deepened. His hands moved uncertainly, wanting to pull the serpent away and stop the throbbing heat that was spreading like liquid fire all through him.

The sorcerer watched him with mocking eyes.

"The Prince of the Deep is on fire with lust," he said, and offered him a flagon made of pink quartz and filled with crushed anemones and tiny bright red and green pebbles. A purple starfish floated on top. "Drink this and you will be a man. But remember, if the prince you desire does not choose you as his mate, you are lost. If he makes a vow of love to another, at the first touch of their bodies, you will die."

Clare took the goblet in his shaking hands and stared at Orcane. For the first time he felt a tremor of doubt. But only for an instant, for surely a grand love such as his would kindle a fire in return? Clare smiled and drank the potion. As the pebbles hit the back of his throat they exploded into peppery licorice, sliding down into his stomach with a sweet scorching fire of their own.

"And now I will take your voice," the sorcerer said, and he cut out Clare's tongue with his flint hard thumbnail.

At that moment, the serpent sank his fangs into Clare's flesh. He tried to scream, but nothing but bubbles escaped from his gaping mouth. Ropes of pain convulsed his body and he trashed about, his mind a blur of agony. The last thing he saw before passing out was the serpent slithering back into the sorcerer's hair.

He awoke on a beach. It was early morning and wisps of fog crept along the sand. He felt very tired, as if he had been swimming for a long time, but he propped himself up on one elbow and looked down at his body. A great joy filled him as he saw two legs and two long delicate feet where his muscular multi-hued tail used to be, and between the legs, nestled in pale gold hair, was a shapely penis, just like the statue's! He fell back with a smile on his face and lay without moving, as the sun touched his skin and slowly burned away the fog. He was a man.

He must have dozed off again, because the next time he opened his eyes, the prince was bending over him. His heart swelled with love as he looked into those midnight eyes at close range for the first time and heard that wonderful resonant voice talking gently to him.

"I'm glad to see you waking up," the Prince was saying. "Can you tell me your name? Where you come from? Certainly not these parts, since I'm sure I would remember anyone as gorgeous as you." The prince smiled down at him and waited, but Clare was unable to utter a sound.

"Perhaps you are struck dumb from some great catastrophe," the prince said at last. "This is almost exactly the spot where I washed up after a storm at sea. It was a miracle, they say. I was found by a beautiful maiden, who looked a lot like you, now that I think on it." He smiled and looked off in the distance, a dreaming expression on his handsome face. Then he shook his head and turned back to Clare. "Come. I'll take you to my palace and look after you, until we can discover what has happened."

The Prince grasped Clare's hand and gently pulled him to his feet. At once, searing pain shot though Clare's body and he gasped, swaying with the shock. The Prince steadied him and wrapped his long velvet cloak around him, so he was not forced to walk naked though the streets to the nearby palace.

Clare was not used to his new body. He found he had to concentrate very hard just to remember to move first one leg, then the other. Every step was agony, but his heart sang to feel the Prince's strong arm around his shoulders and hear his voice talking about how he always took an early morning walk along the beach.

"But this is the first time I have found such a treasure," he said, and Clare thought his heart would break from joy.

When they arrived at the palace, the Prince took Clare to his chambers and gave him silken hose, a shirt of fine linen and a velvet doublet similar to the one he wore.

"A youth so fair must be of royal birth," he said, and he brushed Clare's pale shining hair away from his face, his hand lingering there as those midnight eyes gazed into Clare's.

And Clare tried to put all his love into his sea green eyes, willing the Prince to see what he felt. His throat filled up with words but he was unable to speak.

"Aquamarine," the Prince said softly. "That's what I'll call you."

They spent the day together and that night, the Prince took Clare to the chamber next to his and left him with affectionate words. Clare undressed slowly and climbed into the big four poster bed. He lay still, exhausted from the pain his every step had caused him, trying to hear his prince moving around in the next room. He longed to have the young man beside him, to feel those strong arms around him, a living body to replace the cold marble one he had lain with so often. As the minutes ticked away, his eyes closed and at last he drifted off, lulled by the sound of the waves beneath his window.

A touch awakened him and in the candle light, he saw the Prince in a long white night shirt, gazing down at him anxiously.

"Shh. I did not mean to wake you," he whispered. "I wanted to make sure you were all right after your strenuous day."

Clare gazed at him wordlessly, his green eyes filled with adoration. He flung back the covers and opened his arms to his prince.

Seduced by the pale beauty of Clare's naked body, the prince slipped out of his night shirt and climbed in beside him. He took Clare in his arms and held him tightly, until Clare was afraid he would not be able to breath.

And then a wonderful thing happened. Clare felt a rush of heat gathering between his legs and a tightness began to build there. His new sex organ stiffened of its own accord, straining closer and closer to his bedfellow.

The Prince felt it too and laughed. "You speak quite eloquently at times like this," he said, and his hand moved between them and grasped Clare's organ firmly, stroking its length over and over as Clare began to gasp and groan, shuddering against his Prince as if in the heart of a vast tidal wave down under the ocean. And suddenly, without warning, he erupted, spurting like a geyser all over the hand that stroked him, so that the two of them were almost glued together.

Clare fell back weak with spent passion, his great green eyes drinking in the body beside him.

And then the Prince kissed him and gently scooped up Clare's legs so that they rested over his shoulders. He knelt between them, and anointed his own stiff cock with Clare's essence. He bent close and covered Clare's mouth with his own as slowly, slowly he pushed inside the prince of the Sea. Clare caught his breath. Pain stabbed him, but he clenched his teeth, knowing his Prince wanted this. And then the pain faded away and a great wave of pleasure crashed over him and swept him away. The wave crested then broke again. Clare was panting, watching the Prince's face, shining with sweat as he bucked and drove himself with great slapping thrusts deeper and deeper inside Clare until with a great shout, he emptied his essence and collapsed on top of his mute lover.

Clare thought he would die with happiness.

From that time on, Clare was always with the Prince, day and night, and no one ever guessed what agonies he endured as he moved about, lithe and graceful on feet that were open wounds without blood. The Prince stopped sending out messengers seeking to find out who Clare was. And Clare knew he had found happiness in the land of men.

And then one day a beautiful princess arrived at the court and the Prince gasped with pleasure to see her. She was almost as tall as Clare and her hair was long and pale as sun bleached barley. Her eyes were green though not as luminous and changeable as Clare's. Yet the Prince seemed entranced and Clare's heart was pierced by arrows of jealousy. How could this be, he wondered, and he remembered the words of Orcane and grew very frightened for his life.

That night, the Prince did not come to Clare's bed. Clare stood at the window, looking down to the sea and watched the waves roll in along the crescent of the shore line. Far away he thought he glimpsed the playful splash of one of his siblings. He felt very lonely and afraid. The pain of movement was nothing compared to the ache in his heart.

The next day the Prince spent most of his time with the Princess, and when he was with Clare he talked about her constantly.

"She is the one who found me the time I nearly drowned," he said, his dark eyes dancing. "I have always wanted to see her again!"

But it was I who saved you, Clare wanted to say, but he was mute, forever condemned to silence.

That night and the night after and the night after that Clare lay alone, waiting in vain for his Prince to return. His hand strayed between his legs and discovered the lonely pleasure he gave himself was a sweet accompaniment to his dreams about his beloved. But he longed for the real thing.

After a while, he became a pale shadow of himself, following at a distance while the Prince laughed and talked with the Princess from a far Country. Until at last, one evening, the Prince returned to his bed.

"I wanted you to be the first to know," he said,

sitting beside Clare and taking his hand in his. "Today I asked the Princess to marry me and she accepted. I am a happy man!"

And I am undone, Clare thought, his beautiful eyes filling with tears.

"I see you are so happy for me you are about to weep with joy," the Prince exclaimed. "Thank you, my dearest friend!" And he kissed Clare on the forehead and left the room.

Clare felt a cold stone weighing down his heart. A great sob welled up and caught in his throat. I cannot go on, he thought.

But he did.

The wedding was announced the next day and as time passed, there was great feasting and merry-making in the land. All the time Clare suffered as he moved about, shadowing his beloved as he attended the festivities. And then the great day came and the Princess arrived at the Palace for the ceremony and Clare couldn't stand any more.

He fled to the beach and wandered alone until it was dark. Fire flies darted about, lighting the night. The moon rode high, throwing a silver pathway into the sea. But Clare couldn't follow the pathway home. He no longer had a home.

And then he heard his name, sighing across the water on a gentle breeze and he looked out and saw the Sovereign of the Sea, riding on a giant sea horse.

"My dearest child, there is a way," his father called. "I have visited Orcane and interceded for you. If you kill the Prince before he mates with the Princess, you will live and can return to us again."

Clare sank to his knees. The thought of killing the Prince was more painful than the knives that struck at him every step he took. He nodded and waved and his eyes filled with tears that he couldn't even talk to his parent any more. As he watched, the sea horse leapt up and disappeared in the waves, taking his noble rider with him.

Clare knew that the ceremony and feasting would be almost over by now. Painfully he made his way back to the palace. He wondered what his father had sacrificed to gain this concession from Orcane.

The minstrels still played and sang in the courtyard as he passed and couples still danced as the torches blazed and fireworks exploded above them. Clare paid no attention but made his way up the tower stairs to his chamber. He could hear a soft murmuring coming from behind the door that separated his room from the Prince's apartments. After a moment, he opened the door and slipped inside.

Candles cast a magic glow over the great bed where the Prince lay with the Princess. She was laughing up at him and for a moment, Clare felt blind hatred and wanted to kill her. He took the jewelled dagger from the Prince's belt and crept closer.

"Wait, my Prince. Let me get the unguent from my casket," she said, and suddenly jumped from the bed, trailing diaphanous garments about her, and ran lightly to the dressing chamber.

Clare emerged from the shadows and stood silently beside the bed.

The Prince started on seeing him. "What are you doing here?" he asked.

Clare traced a question mark in the air in front of him.

"Why? But my dearest boy, a prince must marry. If I could follow my heart, perhaps I would marry you." He smiled. "But you know as well as I do the law of the land will not allow such a union."

The stone weighing down Clare's heart grew heavier.

"But I will still come to you at night," the Prince whispered, reaching out to draw Clare closer.

At this, the young Prince of the Sea pulled away and ran back to his own chamber. He flung himself face down on the bed and sobbed, knowing at last that he could never find happiness in the world of men, where there are laws to regulate love.

At last, he got to his feet and took off his velvet clothes and walked naked to the Prince's chamber. He did not look at the bed but kept walking towards the balcony, where the moon beckoned him on. He heard the prince call out to him but he didn't hesitate, moving steadily on his tortured feet out though the door and up onto the wide balustrade. The stone was cool on his bare feet and the night air touched the private places of his body with a damp kiss.

"Wait! Stop!" The Prince rushed out after him, his black hair in disarray, dragging a sheet to cover his nakedness.

Clare looked one last time at his beloved, then turned and plunged to the sea beneath. The water closed over Clare's head. Through the crashing of the surf, he heard his lover's voice:

"No!"

Clare felt a great weight leave his body and for the first time since coming to the land of men, he was free of pain. But in that instant, he felt himself lighten, his mind filling with a vague fog, and he knew he was returning to the sea, dissolving into foam to wash up on the beach as the morning sun rose out of the ocean. Such was death for his kind.

The Prince ignored the cries of his new bride and grabbing his cloak, rushed down to the beach. There was no sign of his young lover. Wrapping his nakedness in the long cloak, the Prince sat down on a rock and cursed the fate that had deprived him of the one he loved. As the sun rose, pale foam washed up on the shore. The Prince gradually immersed himself in the water. On a sudden impulse, he opened his mouth to the foam and let it slide down his throat. The water tasted like tears. He derived a strange comfort from the sensation and lay for a long time, letting the foamy water lap around him until at last, there was nothing left of it at all. He grew cold and went back to the palace where his new bride awaited him.

From that time on, each daybreak found the Prince down on the beach, waiting for the waves to bring him that strange euphoria he had felt on the day his lover returned to the sea.

master

class

I was already sick of my summer job. It didn't do much good to keep telling myself I needed the money for my tuition for music school in the fall. The heat, the humidity, the loneliness of the big unfamiliar city were taking their toll. Day after day I watered and trimmed and repotted in the crowded downtown nursery. Night after night I went home alone, too exhausted to venture out on the town.

By the middle of July, I was about ready to quit in earnest. I had just knocked an expensive ceramic planter off a crowded shelf and was curtly informed that the price would be taken out of my pay. Seething, I bent over the flats of geraniums I was working with, the spicy smell all around me, and rehearsed what I would say to my boss before I flung my gardening gloves in his face and took off for good. I was so into my own anger, I didn't realize I was blocking the narrow walkway until I felt a man's hand on my ass. Surprised, I straightened up abruptly and bumped against a bronzed giant of a man with brilliant green eyes. His strong hands gripped my hips as I swayed in the hot narrow space, dizzy with the heavy scent of the flowers and the physical impact of his look. He was so close I could see the faint sheen of sweat on his upper lip, which was clean shaven, and the tiny crinkles around those wonderful eyes. His face was strong and full of experience. I just knew those eyes had seen far away places.

"Sorry," I stammered. I could still feel the imprint of those fingers through the denim of my cutoffs. I hadn't had a man's hands on me for so long that even this casual contact made me horny.

"I thought I could get by without disturbing you," he said. He made no move to put any distance between us. He appeared unaware of the increasing excitement I was feeling. "Perhaps you could help me," he went on with a smile that seemed meant just for me. "I'm looking for a Ficus to replace the one I've killed with my neglect. I'm not a very good care-giver."

Somehow I doubted that. I was willing to put myself in his care then and there, but aloud I said, "Sure. They're down this aisle."

Reluctantly I turned away from him and led the way past the hanging baskets to the small trees and shrubs, my work boots thumping softly against the packed earth. Although I was not able to see him, I could feel him behind me. I hoped he hadn't noticed my heightened colour.

"I want one that looks just the same," he said, when we had reached the right section. "I'm hoping Ruth won't notice that it's been replaced."

He spent the next ten minutes inspecting different specimens, while I inspected him. He had powerful shoulders and arms, slim hips and wonderfully expressive hands. His white Indian cotton shirt was open almost to his waist and I could see a smooth expanse of well developed hairless chest. His careless sun-bleached hair was longer than I generally liked, but on him it looked good. In the strong light, I could see a touch of silver at the temples. It suited him.

Then I realized he was looking at me with a puzzled frown. I felt the colour rush to my cheeks, afraid he had noticed my obvious arousal. I remembered his mention of Ruth. "Sorry. What did you say?"

"Can you have this delivered before 5 today?"

"Sure. I'll see to it myself."

"Thanks. You've been a big help." He took my hand and shook it before moving back along the narrow aisle and out to the cash register.

I felt a perfectly ridiculous sense of loss. I knew that even if I did see him again, it would do me no good. He was obviously unaware of the feelings his presence inspired in me. Nevertheless, he made me completely reckless. I would do almost anything just to see him again.

A few hours later, my boss expressed surprise when

I appeared before him, eager for the late afternoon deliveries, but he was apparently under the delusion it was due to his earlier lecture on the Work Ethic. I climbed into the dusty pick-up and hurried through the schedule as quickly as possible, leaving the Ficus to the end. There was no name on the label, only an address, a penthouse apartment in an exclusive building overlooking the ravine. It was a surprise to me, for although he had been well dressed, his casual clothing didn't scream money.

On the way up in the purring elevator, I realized I was holding my breath. What for? To him I was just a delivery man. He was married, maybe even had kids... I stopped myself, but it was already too late. Thinking about him in even this negative light gave me a hard-on. The elevator hummed to a stop and I stepped out into the marble entrance hall. There was only one door. When I rang the bell, nothing happened. Disappointment washed over me, cooling me down as efficiently as a cold shower. Evidently I was supposed to leave the tree by the door and go. I had just reached this conclusion, when the door opened and the blond man appeared, fastening the belt of a white terry robe around his waist. His feet were bare, the blond hair matted against his strong calves.

"I was in the shower," he said, pushing back his damp hair with both hands. "Let me help you carry that onto the patio." He bent over to lift one side, and as he did so, his robe opened, making me catch my breath. He was naked, his thick cock dark against the whiteness of the robe. As he moved, it nodded enticingly against his tanned thigh.

He kept talking as we moved through the high ceilinged living room and out onto the huge roof garden beyond. After we set down the heavy tub, I was sweating.

"Have a drink?" He moved to a glass table under an umbrella, picked up the tongs and dropped ice into a glass. "It's sangría. Very cooling."

"Thanks," I said, taking the glass from him.

He refilled his own glass and sat down, not seeming to notice that his robe was open, exposing his magnificent set of genitalia to my hungry gaze. One tanned leg hung casually over the edge of the chair.

I cleared my throat. "Quite a garden you have here," I said, hoping my voice sounded normal.

"Ruth keeps bringing in more and more stuff," he said carelessly. "Every now and then I have to run out and replace something before she notices it's dead." He laughed. "I love plants but frankly I don't have a green thumb."

"Maybe you should subscribe to our plant care service," I said. He nodded absently.

We talked for a few more minutes, me trying desperately to think of things to say that would keep me there longer, him acting more and more as if his thoughts were already elsewhere. At last, I got reluctantly to my feet.

"You're getting quite a burn on your shoulders," I said, looking at the redness where his robe had slipped down.

"Damn! Could you put some lotion on it for me?"

I couldn't believe my luck! I said nothing as I unscrewed the top and squeezed out the colourless cream. Gently I laid my hands against his warm shoulders, feeling a faint shock as my flesh touched his, and spread the cream around. Then I began to knead the knots between his shoulder blades, smoothing them out with my thumbs, working my way down his back. He moaned with pleasure.

"You're good," he said. "You've done this before, haven't you?"

"Yeah. Brian, this guy I used to study with? He'd get real tight after a few hours with the books." I grinned, thinking of the other ways I used to help Brian work out his tension.

I was moving in closer, when he suddenly stood up. I thought I had gone too far, so I was taken totally by surprise when the man reached over and pulled me against him, his strong hands kneading my ass, his mouth sucking at my lips. I could feel his state of arousal and the heat of his body was making me dizzy with lust. My hands pushed under his robe and he caught his breath as I slid down the surprising softness of his stomach.

"God, you're hot," I said. "You're so hot."

"Mmmmm." His tongue was in my ear, driving me crazy when he suddenly pulled away. "Come on," he said. He grabbed my belt and led me inside. We were going down the hall, presumably to the bedroom, when we heard a woman's voice.

"Hello! I'm back. Where are you?"

Without a word, he reached over, opened a door

and pulled me into a closet. It was pitch black when he softly closed the door behind us. Still without saying a word, he pushed me to my knees and guided my head to his crotch. I took his swollen cock in my eager mouth and sucked, licked along the shaft, nibbled the distended bud. In the dark, all my senses were concentrated on his taste, his smell, the feel and heat of his sun-bronzed body. I heard the rustle of his robe as it slid off his shoulders, felt the soft whoosh of air as it slipped to the floor. He was leaning against the wall, cushioned by the clothes that hung there, his legs far apart to give me room. His hands were in my hair, tugging and pulling and patting. His laboured breathing filled the small space, mingling with the slurp and suck of my mouth against his bulging cock. I slid my tongue underneath him, wetting his balls, licking up the salty taste of him, filling my mouth with his soft hairy sacks. When I pulled back to get my breath, I heard the woman walk past on the other side of the door. His fingers clenched in my hair and I lunged forward again, filling my mouth with his hot flesh to stop myself from crying out. I felt his body tense, his breathing shorten into quick gasps. My hands slid up and grabbed his ass, pushing him into me. He was pumping now, fucking my face like his life depended on it. It was weird, the absolute darkness, the hot stifling confines of the small space, the effort at silence. As I brought him to climax, his knees almost gave way and I drained him, gulping down his hot juice in an ecstasy of pleasure.

Gasping, he pulled me to my feet and fumbled with my belt. I helped him, and still without a word, we went at it again, this time with him on his knees and my fingers in his hair. I was so horny, I came almost at once and sank exhausted into his arms. For a few moments, we held onto each other, our breath finally evening out.

Then he kissed me.

"I don't even know your name," I whispered, sensing that our adventure was almost over.

"Morgan," he said.

"I'm Tim."

He seemed to listen for a moment, one hand on the back of my neck. "I think she's gone. Let's get out of here before we die of suffocation."

The sunlight almost blinded me when he opened the door and stepped out into the hall, shrugging into his robe. He glanced at his watch, then headed for the living room and the front door.

"Thanks for the drink," I said, and then wished I hadn't.

He just laughed.

As the elevator doors slid together, his brilliant green eyes held mine for one last minute. Then he was gone.

For days I couldn't get the man out of my mind. At night I would think of him while my hands tried to drown the fever his image brought over me. Even my music didn't help.

Then one day I was in the music store walking through the classical section on my way upstairs to the jazz area, when I saw that face looking out at me from a jacket cover. Morgan! Astonished, I stopped and read the notes. 'Well known concert pianist who has toured extensively in Europe and South America, Morgan Rostand is now turning to recording', the notes informed me.

So that explained the strength of the hands, the well developed shoulders. A pianist, like myself. Well, in a different field, not to mention a different class, but the same instrument anyway. Naturally I bought the CD and listened to it all evening. The crashing harmonies excited me almost as much as the man who played them. I began to think of going back to the study of classical music. But how I longed for the touch of the master's hands!

A week later I had developed a sort of ritual. I spent an hour with my keyboards, not plugged in, naturally, since the neighbours would complain, then put on Morgan's CDs and lay on the bed with my pants off, masturbating to the music. Unsatisfactory as this was, it was the closest I could get to what I wanted.

I was in the middle of this rite one evening, when a knock came at the door, I scrambled into my shorts fast and turned down the music. Some neighbour complaining again, I thought angrily. For the third time this week!

I flung open the door, ready to fight.

"Does my playing make you that angry?" Morgan said.

I was speechless. Finally I backed into the room. "How did you find me?"

"Nothing terribly esoteric. I asked your boss."

"Why?"

For answer, he walked over and took me in his arms. His hands soon peeled off my shorts and pushed me back on the bed. In another moment he was naked himself, pushing my legs back, licking along my ass crack until he found my hole, lubricating it with his mouth. One strong finger found its way inside me, then another.

"Oh, shit! Oh Morgan! Fuck me!"

"Why do you think I came over here?" he muttered, pushing my legs onto his shoulders.

He slid into me carefully at first, the hot bud of his cock pushing just inside and staying there, teasing me with little forward motions, then almost withdrawing. I wrapped my legs around his sturdy body, lifting my hips, trying to draw him deeper inside me. But he knew what he was doing and went on, driving me mad with desire, my cock dribbling onto my chest. He built his rhythm slowly and at last, he was driving into me, pounding his balls against my ass, rocking my bed so that it hit the wall behind my head, over and over again. We didn't care. We laughed and shouted and gasped, until we finally came, almost together.

"Oh God! That was so good!" I cried.

"I never did like closet sex!"

My neighbour pounded on the wall. Morgan pounded back. We laughed until the tears came and then I licked them off his cheeks. And kept going, lingering on his hard nipples. He had a small scar just over the left one that felt rough to my tongue.

"I want you again," he said. And he took me, hard and hot, so that my hole was sore and my muscles quivering from exhaustion. And I loved it!

Finally he stopped to rest. I lay beside him, smelling our mingled sweat, and cupped his balls gently in my hand.

"I kept thinking about you," Morgan said. "For a while I thought your image would go away. It didn't. As soon as I got back to town, I came to get you."

"What about Ruth?" I said.

"What about her?" Then he laughed. "She's my agent! What did you think?"

I punched him on the arm and laughed too, weak with relief.

Morgan was looking around the room, taking in the keyboards, the sheet music, the CDs. "You're a musician," he said, sounding surprised.

"I'm still working on it," I said modestly.

"You want a master class?" he said, his green eyes looking down into my soul.

And that is how I came to live with Morgan Rostand. And, incidently, how come I play both jazz and classical gigs. I don't go on tour much. I don't want to be away from Morgan that long. And I always remember to water the plants!

sexual

warrior

The black water slid around Micah's naked body like liquid ice. It took his breath away. He stood perfectly still, gasping for air, and waited for his limbs to go numb. The water was up to his armpits. Frigid. Paralysing. His teeth began to chatter. Nothing in his years as a Nebula Warrior, nothing in his more recent training from his alien master Attlad, had prepared him for the bone-chilling dread that seeped into him now. Across the inky blackness of the water loomed the Cave of Truth, where his worth as a witness on behalf of his beloved master would be tested. Was it myth, or reality, this secret ritual place of Kudite mystery and magic? When he turned his head, his guide had already disappeared. There was no time left for questions.

Micah began to swim. It was awkward holding his bundle of cloths out of the water, but he had had practice doing this in his years as a soldier. It was only the terrible cold that he was not prepared for in this shadowed alien place. It seemed to take forever for that lifegiving tingle to work its way through his veins, letting him know he was alive after all. He swam steadily towards the menacing darkness. His naked body barely caused a ripple in the inky water.

As he drew into the shadow of the cave, he thought about how he had trusted his life to his guide, this young alien male he had met only two nights ago. And yet, he had little choice. He was a wanted man. At least dying here would be more worthy of a soldier, he thought wryly, then being hunted down and tortured to death by his arch enemy Kerdas. This way, he would die trying to save his master's honour, and that was a worthy goal.

His foot scraped against rock and he realized he was inside the mouth of the cave. Before him, the ground rose abruptly, so that he was on dry land a few feet inside the entrance. He was shivering so much it was difficult to get his clothes back on, but finally he was ready. The small hand torch cast just enough light to throw wavering shadows high on the uneven rock-face as he started his journey deeper into the cave.

Suddenly, a tall man with long hair was before him. It was hard to tell in the dim light what age he was, but something about him spoke of experience and ancient wisdom. He held a long staff with a pale green light glowing at the top end.

"I am Micah Starion," the Terran said at once. "I am a stranger, come to ask your help." e held his hands in the available light, hoping the man could read the sign language he had been taught.

"No one comes to the Cave of Truth hiding his body, hiding his trust."

"Forgive me if I do not know the customs here, sir. The clothes are for warmth, not to conceal."

The man didn't reply. The longer Micah stood there, facing the silent figure whose features he was unable to see with any clarity, the more he felt the weight of that disapproval. Then the feeling changed. It was almost disappointment, verging towards disgust, that Micah felt in the air around him. And not only from one man, but from a group. There were more than just the two of them in the Cave, he realized. Alarm jolted through him and it took all his willpower to remain calm.

He began to take off his clothes, his skin breaking out in gooseflesh as the chill hit his nakedness. Beneath his fear was an undercurrent of anger that he was being reduced once again to the status of a naked slave, not because he had chosen the role, but because it was demanded of him. He didn't even have the long blond hair on his head to cover him now, since he had been completely shaved when he arrived at the Citadel. As his pants dropped to the ground, he was aware of an odd current of air swirling around his feet, like a door being opened, letting in a draft. He shivered, lifting his feet free of the clothes. Then, it was if the clothes simply disappeared. Startled, he looked down, but could see nothing. It was as if there had never been anything there.

He cleared his throat. "I am ready for any tests you may wish to give me," he said, signing the words as well, though he had the strong feeling communication in this place had no need of words.

"Why are you here?"

The question was a surprise. He had somehow assumed that these dwellers in the Cave of Truth were all-knowing. Perhaps it meant that they wanted him to express his purpose. He wrapped his arms around himself, trying to still the shivering that shook his body. His skin felt clammy and his own touch did little to warm him. He raised his head, feeling the damp air cling to his shaved scalp. He began to tell the story of Attlad's unjust arrest for a murder that Micah himself had committed to save his master from a traitorous attack. "I was told that the only way I can testify for him and stand any chance of being believed, is if I pass through your Cave of Truth," he finished.

"What do you expect from us?" The question hovered in the air before him.

Micah drew in his breath and squared his shoulders. "I'm not sure," he said truthfully. "I don't really understand it, but it's something to do with testing my integrity." He paused, looking for the right word. He had a sudden vivid memory of Attlad's father and the awe with which his visions and dreams were reported and studied. "I give you my dreams as evidence of my good faith," he said.

"Your soul."

"I will show you my soul," he said, "in my dreams." For the first time, he sensed approval from the unseen men around him. Suddenly, he was no longer freezing.

"Your dreams are the dreams of a warrior— and a sex slave, since you are both."

"I do not come here as a slave," Micah protested. Unconsciously he threw back his broad shoulders and raised his head challengingly.

"But you are both. There is no shame in being a sexual warrior."

The term sounded odd to Micah, but if that was how they looked at things, it was fine by him. Now that he thought of it, it was a very apt term to describe his life with Attlad, a life that seemed very far away at the moment.

In front of him, the tall shadowy figure moved deeper into the cave. His pale hand beckoned Micah to follow. This time, there seemed to be no need of a torch. His bare feet walked unerringly over the smooth beaten earth floor, as long as he kept his eyes on the moving shadow in front of him. Once, he turned his head, trying to get a clearer picture of his surroundings. Instantly, he stumbled. Around him, he felt that surge of disapproval again, as if he had failed some sort of test. The feeling of being watched, returned. His cock stiffened slightly.

The ground had been rising steadily, along with the temperature. His navigator's mind knew they were now well above the level of the cave opening. The floor under his feet no longer felt like pounded earth, but was more like smooth marble. Ahead of him, a pale light reflected off the gleaming wall. They were coming to some sort of a chamber. The path veered to the right. Turning the corner, he stopped in surprise.

Before him was a vast chamber filled with a green glow. The light glistened along slender icicles of crystal, thick as a man's arm, that hung from the vaulted ceiling almost to the glass-smooth floor. The walls were pebbled with mirror-like bits of black, that refracted the light back in tiny jewelled shards that dazzled his eyes, making him unsure of what he was really seeing. He had a fleeting impression of a group of tall male figures around the edges of the space, but when he looked closer, the image vanished, replaced by the green lights, dancing with the shadows. When he looked back to his guide, he saw a young man, standing before him in a ray of light. His long robe was open and he was naked underneath.

"Stand over there." The man's voice was deep, filling the great space, yet quiet and firm.

Micah walked to the area between two giant icicles, and stood on a sort of platform.

"Now, tell us, in your own words, why you have made this journey."

Micah began to talk, slowly at first, unsure whether or not he was being understood. When it became clear that they knew what he was saying, he was soon caught up in his own tale, trying to lay it all out before them in as clear and unbiased a way as possible. When he finished, there was a long silence.

"We understand what you have told us," the guide

said. "We hear the words of the warrior. Now, show us your soul. Take hold of the crystal pillars, stretching as high as you can on either side."

Micah did as he was told, aware that many unseen eyes were devouring his naked body. He found pleasure in the warmth of their gaze. He stood easily between the columns, legs apart, as he had been taught. As he reached high above his head and touched the rough surface of the stalactites, he was startled to find he could no longer move his hands. He was held as captive as if he were shackled in chains to the pillars. When he tried to shift his feet, he found it impossible.

"Is this your idea of a sexual warrior?" he cried, pulling against his invisible bonds. No amount of writhing could loosen them, however. He was securely imprisoned, hanging on display, bathed in the unearthly green light.

He felt, rather than saw, the others gather around him, felt the touch of male hands on his body. Cool fingers grazed against his skin, lingering on the welts and scars left by Kerdas's whip, and as each one was touched, it flamed alive and pain jolted through him anew. He clenched his teeth, holding the hurt inside, willing it through his body. Each re-opened wound brought with it the memory of how and when it was inflicted, and he relived the intense experience again, and again. As the hands moved over him, as the lash bit through his skin anew, Micah screamed and cried out and cursed until his throat was raw, his muscles strained and aching and his mind afire with agony.

And then a hand touched his cock. His eyes sprang

open and he looked into the jet black eyes of his guide, and he saw there the image of Attlad, holding him in his arms while his master's symbol, the red dragon, was tattooed on his cock. At once he felt a shock of pleasure so intense, he thought he would come. He looked down to see his cock jutting out from his naked crotch, the dragon proud and rampant.

"Attlad," said his guide, recognizing the war lord's emblem.

Micah was now totally confused, as the men withdrew their touch, leaving him without feeling, his cock aching, his asshole throbbing, sucking at the empty air. He felt tears in his eyes for the first time. All the pain was as nothing to this desolation. His chest heaved as the longing surged through him.

Then, without warning, he was free. He staggered, supporting himself against the pillar with one hand. For the first time he saw the other men, walking away from him in single file, a long line of men, naked except for a bright chain looped over one shoulder and crossing to hang against the opposite hip like a bandolier. The metal links caught the light and glittered, the brilliance hurting his eyes. When the last man had reached the centre of the room, his guide joined the line. As if on a signal, Micah fell into step behind him.

As the file progressed through the cavern, a swell of sound rose up around them. It was faint, at first, like the breaking of waves upon a distant shore; then grew louder as the long column wound its way through the maze of crystal stalactites and into another chamber, beyond.

Micah moved to the centre of the area and walked up the short flight of steps there. The others formed a circle around him. Once again he was bathed in the strange green light, shining down on him like a spotlight from directly above. Without being told, he again placed his hands on the stalactites on either side of his small platform and stood immobile, his feet apart, firmly attached by the unseen bonds.

Then the circle wavered and broke. As the strange sounds swirled around them, one man approached Micah and stood in front of him, his mouth on a level with the Terran's still engorged cock. Closing his eyes, he took Micah's cock into his mouth in one smooth motion, sucking it down his throat. Micah threw back his head and moaned. The wonderful sensations purred around his eager cock, the throat muscles working it skilfully until he came in a burst of pent-up passion. The music crashed around him. At once, the man opened his eyes, slid the deflating cock out of his mouth and rejoined the circle.

Immediately, the next man took his place and repeated the process. Micah shook and moaned with pleasure as yet again, he came. When the third man took the wilting meat in his mouth, Micah protested, but to no avail. There was no way to stop the process, which was fast becoming an insidious torture as his nuts were sucked dry again. And again. And again. It took longer and longer, but somehow, each man brought him to shuddering orgasm, until even the thought of his cock getting hard, made him whimper. It was then that the guide approached him.

"No!" cried Micah. "Oh God, not again!"

The man in front of him raised his hand in an imperious gesture. His face now seemed ageless, his pale skin taut over well-toned muscles. Micah felt his protest die in his throat. The odd swell of sound retreated. In the silence, the sudden movement of the men in the circle unnerved him. There was a crash, followed by a juddering clatter as gold chains slid off broad shoulders, the links clinking together. Micah shuddered, the noise set his teeth on edge. Goose bumps brook out on his skin. As if at a signal, the men took the chains in their right hands and swung them towards their neighbour. As the left hands caught the bright links, a true circle formed joining the men and the chains. In some way Micah didn't understand, the atmosphere thickened, as if all the energy of the place were gathered right here in the circle around him.

Once again his invisible bonds released him. The air condensed around him, pressing against him, lifting him up, up, until he was immersed in the soft green light, suspended above the circle, his arms and legs still spread wide. He looked down and saw the guide, his right arm held high. His palm began to move backwards, as if he were balancing a tray above his head. Gradually Micah's body tilted until he lay as if on a board in the middle of the cave. Gradually he descended until he felt the cool hard pressure of smooth stone against his back. He realized he had been holding his breath. He began to pant, short, hard puffs of air that rasped in his throat. His heart knocked in his chest. His body dripped with sweat. They were playing tricks with his mind, he told himself. That's all it was. Mind games, like they used to do with young cadets at the Academy, like Attlad did to him back at the complex. But reason could not hold on to what was happening here. Reason itself slid away as he fought to get his breath, to move his hands down from above his head. Who were these people?

The low wail of the eerie music started up again as the guide came into his line of vision. Now he was carrying something in front of him on a tray, but Micah couldn't make out what it was. The light gleamed on the man's muscular body, bringing out the lines of his biceps, his pectorals. His cock was thick, half hard in its nest of coarse black hair. Micah licked his lips and looked up at the man's impassive face.

Candles. They were small votive candles on the tray and the leader, as Micah now thought of him, began to place them on Micah's prone body. Everywhere the small cylinders of wax touched his skin he felt a tiny shock. This at least was something he understood. His breathing evened out. His muscles jumped in anticipation. He clenched and unclenched his fists.

The leader slid the tray out of sight underneath the stone table. He leaned over Micah, his black eyes glittering, refracting the green light as if they were jewels. Suddenly, the candles were lit, how he didn't understand. The tiny flames danced over the Terran's helpless body and he watched as the wax began to melt, pooling next to the burning wicks, ready to spill over onto his naked flesh if he moved. He swallowed hard.

Little sparks of sexual tension danced just under his skin, making his tits stand out. His cock began to stiffen. No! Micah tried to will it back to its flaccid state. He had had too much. The pain of his erection would shake through his body, leaving splashes of melted wax to burn new scars against his flesh.

Control. Breathe carefully. Keep it shallow so no breath would move his chest, holding the candles perfectly still. Micah watched each tiny flame, mesmerized as the melting pools grew deeper, larger, until finally the inevitable happened. Scalding wax slid over onto his body. Small jolts of pain seared his belly, his left groin, his right nipple. He clenched his jaw, determined to keep in control. He had taken much more severe assaults on his body than this.

From the corner of his eye, he saw the leader slide the heavy gold chain off his shoulder. The metal seemed to slither down his arm. The Kudite moved to the foot of the table and stood there, arms outstretched, the gleaming chain held with both great hands. Micah stared at him through the golden haze of the candles, his vision blurred by pain. Although his head was not restrained in any way, he couldn't look away, rivetted by the tall imposing figure who now slid the gold links of the chain onto the slab of rock. The ed with a soft hiss into three separate parts. Micah felt the scream rise in his throat as the golden snakes reared up for a moment and then slithered between his legs. His body spasmed with fear, sending rivulets of liquid pain spilling across his chest, his belly, his shaved groin. A low moan escaped from his throat, rising higher in short gasps as the creatures undulated up onto his thighs. There were three or four of them, their dry scaly bodies sending odd shivers across the surface of Micah's skin as they reared up and looked about, their thin red tongues darting in and out as if in search of prey. Their jewel-like eyes glittered.

Another gasp sent more wax searing onto his skin. His cock was hard. Attlad's red dragon stood up tall and proud and the snakes turned slowly, their cold stares watching intently. The closest one struck first. Its teeth, razor sharp, sent needle-like stabs into his cock. Micah began to struggle at last. Terror and pain overcame all rational thought. His screams cut through the air as the wax slid over his skin, coating his body in heat. The snakes reacted with a concerted attack on his cock, that was now rock hard. Then one snake wrapped its scaly body around his penis. Arching his back, Micah's scream turned into a long wail of ecstasy as he came in great arcing spurts, over and over and over again. He wouldn't have thought it possible, after what he had been through, but the long strings of creamy liquid were proof enough that this was real. When it was over, he collapsed back on the rock, spent. As his eyes refocused, he saw the snakes loop around each other as they slid off his crotch and reformed into a chain. He closed his eyes.

The rock beneath him shuddered and began to move. His eyes sprang open in terror as the stone slab he was fastened to with invisible bonds, rose towards the vaulted ceiling of the cave, gathering speed as it went. The air rushed past his ears. Green light exploded in brightness, almost blinding him. And then, with a great crash, everything went black.

The next thing he knew, he was outside. Rain poured down around him in sheets, but he himself remained dry. Forked lightening split the sky. Thunder crashed and rumbled in the distance. Micah jerked to a sitting position, surprised to find he was free. His wax-splattered nakedness gleamed an unearthly blue in the flash of the lightning.

Suddenly, the rain stopped.

"Are you ready to go back and free your master?"

The young Kudite guide, who had brought him to this place, stood beside the rock table, his green eyes steady on Micah's face. In his arms were the clothes the Terran had shed back in the Cave.

Micah pushed back the rush of questions that raced through his mind. One thing at a time, he reminded himself. What was it they had called him? A sexual warrior? He liked that. He liked that a lot.

"I'm ready," he said.

(excerpt from the novel *The Citadel,* the sequel to *The Initiation of P.B. 500*)

✝✝

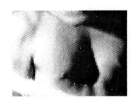

Coming in 2001

February 2001:

The Abulon Dance by Caro Soles ISBN: 0-9686776-2-2
While on tour to mysterious Abulon, the pleasure-loving
hermaphrodite dancers of Merculian are intrigued by the
virile patriarchal society they discover there. But when the
star's young lover is kidnapped, they find themselves
plunged into an alien civil war that they are ill equipped to
survive. Only the love of the young Abulonian heir for one
of the rebel soldiers offers them hope, but can this inexperi-
enced youth prevail against his father's troops?
 †† gay fantasy/adventure

September 2001

The Initiation of P.B. 500, by Kyle Stone
At last! A new edition of Stone's startling debut novel—
the long out-of-print SM/SF cult classic. Volume One of
the infamous adventures of the warrior/slave Chento and
his alien master, Attlad, will be available from The Back
Room in September 2001.
 †† gay sf/sm adventure ~ erotica

Check the web page for details:
www.baskervillebooks.com